Praise for *Joe All Alone*

"Poignant, funny, and utterly unputdownable,
Joe All Alone paints a picture ... that is somehow
life-affirming and heart-warming – even while it
will break your heart."
Catherine Bruton, author of *I Predict a Riot*
and *We Can Be Heroes*

"A real boy's voice, nailed hard to a tale
rich with wrong decisions, hopeless plans
and stabs at redemption. I loved it."
Steve Cole

"Frightening and funny, bleak and tender,
serious and surprising, *Joe All Alone* is a gem of a
book that catches the heart and lifts the spirits
(just like a flock of parakeets in Peckham!)"
Tanya Landman

Joe All Alone

Joanna Nadin

LITTLE, BROWN BOOKS FOR YOUNG READERS
www.lbkids.co.uk

For the two Joes

LITTLE, BROWN BOOKS FOR YOUNG READERS

First published in Great Britain in 2015 by Hodder & Stoughton

1 3 5 7 9 10 8 6 4 2

Text copyright © Joanna Nadin, 2015

The moral right of the author has been asserted.

A CIP catalogue record for this book
is available from the British Library.

ISBN 978-0-349-12455-1

Typeset in Bembo by M Rules
Printed and bound in Great Britain by
Clays Ltd, St Ives plc

The paper and board used in this book are made from
wood from responsible sources.

MIX
Paper from
responsible sources
FSC® C104740
www.fsc.org

Little, Brown Books for Young Readers
An imprint of
Hachette Children's Group
Part of Hodder & Stoughton
Carmelite House
50 Victoria Embankment
London EC4Y 0DZ

An Hachette UK Company
www.hachette.co.uk

www.hachettechildrens.co.uk

Friday 24 May

I should know something's up right from the off, because when I get in Dean isn't on the sofa playing Xbox, there's just that big dip there instead and a stain from where he spilt Cherry 20/20 that time. And Mum has this smile on her like she's on a TV game show, all stretched so wide you think her face is going to crack. And then she gives me a Mars bar and we haven't had them in yonks. But my head's too busy being happy that it's the last day of school, which means no Perry Fletcher for a whole week, and that I get a chocolate bar instead of a biscuit or bread and marg, and that I can play Xbox without getting kicked off or kicked. So it's not until Dean comes back four hours later with his breath all sour and two plane tickets in his hand that I know any better.

"Think of it like a holiday," Mum says.

And I try, but I can't. Because there are too many other thoughts all saying stuff like, *Who goes on holiday to Peckham? To their own flat? Not anyone I know, that's for sure. Stacey Hale went to Disneyland last Christmas. And Kyle Hoskins went to Malaga yesterday with his mum and stepdad, even though Mr Pruitt sent a letter home saying it was breaking school rules when they did it in the summer.*

"Why can't I come with you?" I ask.

She looks down, starts scratching at a patch of dried-out tinned spaghetti. "We can't afford it, love," she says. Then she looks up again. "And Dean's got a little job while we're out there. You don't want to be hanging around while he's working, do you."

I shrug and wonder what she'll be doing when Dean's working, and what the little job actually is. If it's carrying bricks like he does sometimes for Chinese Tony, or something else.

Then I remember something Bradley said, about when his mum and dad went to see his Aunty Reenie in Cyprus that time. "Nan could come," I say. "She could stay here and look after me."

"Don't be daft." Mum tries to laugh, but it comes out all mangled, like a choking noise.

"I'm not. I just don't get—" But I don't finish the sentence because Dean has got something to say. Dean's always got something to say.

"You don't need your nan. You don't need anyone. It's only a week and you're thirteen not flaming three." He's back in the hollow on the sofa with his Bensons and his beer and the joystick in his hands. He shoots at something and ash falls from a cigarette on to his crotch. "Christ, when I

3

was your age I was living in the caravan, working down the pier and smoking twenty a day."

Mum swears at him when he says that but Dean just laughs. "Welcome to the real world, son."

I'm not your son, I think. *And it's not up to you, it's up to Mum.*

But that's not true and we all know it.

"Dean's right, love. You'll be OK, won't you?"

She's up in my face now, so close I can see those pores like little pinholes in her nose where I used to think the rain would get in. And I can smell that her breath is sour too and see her smile is thinner. And I know she needs more than anything for me to say yes so I say it.

"OK."

"Good boy."

And when she says that I feel a rush of warmth in my stomach like syrup on Ready Brek and I know I've done the right thing.

And the more I think about it now the more I reckon it's like being in a book or a film or something. Like I'm Tom Sawyer. Or Huckleberry Finn even, all on my own, lighting out for the territory. Mum read me that book three times even though it's 368 pages long. She wasn't keen because it took three months to do them all but I begged and begged and in the end she gave in. Only the book got taken to the charity shop with my old clothes when we moved here because Dean said if I'd already heard it all what was the point of keeping it. Mum hasn't read me anything since but Dean says that's because I'm not a little kid.

And Dean's right: I'm not a little kid, I'm not three, I'm thirteen, just like Huck was, so I don't need a babysitter. And everyone at school says this kid Dane Fenwick was on his own in Chelsea House for two days when his mum had Letisha and that was when we were only eleven. Plus it's just for a week. That's only five days more than Dane. And they'll back in the blink of an eye, Mum said. Back before I know it.

It'll be like an adventure, she said.

A holiday and an adventure.

Only without the Mississippi or a boat or Tom Sawyer at my side.

Saturday 25 May (7 days left)

They go at five in the morning to get the plane and I'm too tired and there's too much shouting and packing and panicking to say goodbye properly. But then, when they're nearly out the door, Mum flies back in, Dean trying to grab her like she's one of the Dooleys' Staffies running off after a cat. "There's just one rule," she says. "You can't tell anyone. It's our secret."

"Why?" I say.

Mum shakes Dean off and he swears again, but

quiet, so's the old guy in the flat opposite doesn't wake up and want to know what's going on.

"Not everyone will understand," she says. "Not everyone will think you're old enough. Not everyone knows you're ... special."

"Special flaming needs," mutters Dean. But I ignore him like Mum always tells me to.

"Promise me," Mum says.

I pick a crust of sleep out the corner of my eye. "All right," I say. "I promise."

"And don't answer the phone," adds Dean.

"Why not?" I say, panicked.

"Because I say so."

"Dean ... " Mum gives him a look.

"What if you need to ring me? Say if—" I rack my brains "—if the flight back's delayed or something."

Mum starts before Dean can get in. "If we need to call, we'll call at, say, six exactly, OK?" She's looking at Dean not me.

Dean looks back at her like she's retarded but he

agrees anyway 'cause they're late and he can always change his mind, can't he.

"Whatever. But only at six, right. And while you're at it, no drink and no girls."

"What?"

He laughs. "You heard me."

"Jesus, Dean." Mum pulls a *sorry* look at me.

Dean ignores it. "I know what I was like at his age."

"Yeah, well, he's not like you. Are you, Joe?"

I shake my head. I am nothing like him. Not one cell of my body, not one atom of me.

"Don't I know it." Dean smiles, only not the good kind, the kind when someone knows something you don't. The kind Perry Fletcher does when he's stuck something on your back or in your locker or told Lacey Barton that you fancy her even though she smells of dog and damp.

I think he's about to say something else then, something worse. But Mum gets in the way to give me another hug and then he's pulling her off and down the stairs and they're gone. And the flat is empty, and silent save for the hum of the fridge in the corner.

And then I'm awake. More awake than I've ever been, as if there's electricity instead of blood in my veins like I'm some kind of superhero. Because I feel it, what this means: that I'm on my own now. I'm Joe Holt and I'm all alone.

At first I sit very still in the hollow on the sofa, like I can't move with the weight of it. But then it starts to build up inside me; the electricity is too much and suddenly I'm up and jumping on the cushion like a kid, then on to the floor and I let out this whoop, this rebel yell, until the Polish woman underneath bangs on the ceiling with her broom and I remember about the secret and I flop down on the sofa again, my heart bang-banging loud enough to drown out the fridge.

I'm on my own. I'm on my own and it feels good.

*

It's amazing what you can do when no one's there to tell you you can't, or you shouldn't, or if you do then you're just flaming mental. Like, for breakfast I have a Mars bar, a packet of Hula Hoops and half a tin of peaches, which is one of my five a day so I don't feel too bad about the other stuff. And I figure I can have cereal for tea anyway so it'll all even out in the end. And who decided what you eat when anyway? Dean probably. Though I've seen him eat a kebab at six in the morning once so he's not that clever.

Anyway, the point is, Dean's not here, which means I can eat what I want and watch what I want on telly, so I watch *Man versus Food*, which is where this guy Adam Richman tries to eat the world's biggest pizza for instance without chucking up, only this time it's ice-cream cake called Death by Chocolate and I start to feel a bit sick from the Mars bar so I switch over to *Homes Under the Hammer* and decide which house we're going to live in when I'm old enough to have a job. I pick a three-bed terrace in somewhere called Larkhall because every bedroom has its own sink so's I'd never have to share with Dean who leaves shaving stuff in ours, and once he peed in it when the toilet was blocked. Plus from the window of the house you can see this big hill in the distance, covered in trees like Middle Earth in that film *Lord of the Rings* or something. It would be good to live in Middle Earth instead of Peckham. All you can see from our windows is the bus stop outside Crackerjack, the roof of the Wishing Well pub where Dean goes, and the Prince Albert where he doesn't because he's barred. Mum says it's what you make of somewhere that matters, but she didn't grow up here, she's from Cornwall. I've Googled it and it looks a bit like *Lord of the Rings* too, only with beaches and clotted cream and girls with tans that don't come out of a bottle.

It would be better if there was someone good who lived in the flats; someone to hang out with. But they're mostly old or foreign, and Dean doesn't like us talking to people like that. Like on the ground floor is this big black woman called Mrs Joyful King. I only know her name because I've seen a magazine for her stuck in the letterbox. And opposite her are some Polish men only it's never the same Polish men, it changes every month. On the second floor is an empty flat and some students who aren't old or foreign but Dean says you can't trust them because they have beards and their trousers are too tight. Then there's the Patels who have kids only they keep themselves to themselves, and the old Polish woman. Then on the top floor is us and the old black guy. He smiles and says hello and when he does you can see he has three gold teeth. But I don't usually say anything back. Dean says it's better that way or everyone starts poking their nose into your business.

Even Dean hates it here. It's about the one thing we agree on. That and that Man United are overrated.

I think about what he said then, about staying away from girls, and I think chance would be a fine thing. Bradley says he's kissed fourteen girls now, including Caz Beasley who's in Year 10 and has 34C breasts, which is a good size according to him. He says he touched one once only it was through her jumper and shirt and bra which I don't think counts but he says what do I know. He's probably right. I've not even held hands with a girl unless you count in country dancing at primary, which I don't, because it was Letitia Betts and her palms were all sweaty.

I know I should turn the telly off, because I've already watched seven hours, which is more than even Bradley does in one go. If Mum was here, she'd say to get out from under her feet and get some fresh air and see Bradley or Mason Venning who I used to hang out with before big school. But Mason got sent to Fourways for headbutting Mr Dimitri. And Bradley mostly hangs out with

Perry Fletcher these days. I don't know why, because Perry spent most of Year 6 tripping me and Bradley up and calling me a gay mentalist for washing my hands before and after lunch and sometimes after class too, which is quite common according to Dr Khalil but not according to Perry. And once he stuck Bradley's bag down a toilet and when we got it out it had paper stuck to it and everything and next day he had to use a Morrison's carrier.

Maybe that's why. 'Cause at least he doesn't get that any more. Perry's going to end up in Fourways too if you ask me. The sooner the better. Though it'll probably be me he headbutts to get in there.

Anyway, Mum's not here and nor are her feet to get under so I might as well stay in and play Xbox. I could play it all afternoon if I wanted. Even all night. I could set a new world record for the most hours playing, say, Grand Theft Auto, in a row. Only I don't know what the actual record is because I can't Google it because Mum spilt Coke on the laptop and the screen went black and Dean went mental though I don't know why because he didn't even pay for it, he got it off Gerry Finn down the Wishing Well in exchange for an Alsatian puppy called Fritz, which he got off the Dooleys in exchange for something else Mum won't tell me about.

I did about nine hours I think, not including the times I got up to get crisps and Cheestrings or to pee. The person who has the record must have some kind of special system so's he can pee in a bottle hidden inside his trousers. That or he wears a giant nappy. It's weird what thoughts you have when nobody's about to interrupt them with farting or swearing or trying to burp the National Anthem.

At some point I must have fallen asleep though because it's gone one in the morning and the only light is the weird glow from the TV screen. I should turn it off so's I don't waste electricity because it costs a tenner every time Mum has to recharge the key and she has to do that twice a week as it is. She's left me twenty pounds for one recharge plus emergencies. I asked her what sort of emergency might happen and she said if she knew that it wouldn't be an emergency because they're things you can't predict like hurricanes or tidal waves or a tiger on the loose. I said a tenner wasn't going to be enough in that case. But Dean said if any of those emergencies actually happened I'd be brown bread anyway i.e. dead, so money wouldn't be an issue so to keep my mouth shut before he shut it for me.

I've turned the TV off but I'm going to keep the hall light on. Because what if someone thinks we're all away, not just Mum and Dean, and tries to burgle us? That happened to Ali Hassan's mum two years ago. She woke up with two men in hoodies in her bedroom trying to get her gold jewellery. She hit one of them with the crowbar that's by the bed but not before they'd smashed her nose in. I don't want my nose smashed so I'm keeping the light on. And I don't care if Dean says I'm a spaz for being scared, because Dean's not here.

Sunday 26 May (6 days left)

My eyes and hands hurt and I'm like a snail or a sloth or that kid called Jamil in Year 10 who's clinically obese and goes everywhere in slow motion. I feel like I did after Mum's friend Jeanie married Gary Menzies down the Liberal Club and I ate too many Jammie Dodgers and did karaoke until one in the morning. Not a hangover though like Mum had because you need Lambrini or cider for that and I'm not touching them. Mum says Lambrini's the only reason Jeanie married Gary in the first place, and now they're divorced and she goes out with one of the Dooleys so it's obviously bad for you. My mouth tastes weird too and when I looked in the mirror there was fur on my tongue and I realised I hadn't brushed my teeth last night either.

I'm going to be sensible today i.e. no watching TV for hours or playing Xbox all night or eating chocolate for breakfast. Because that's the point, isn't it? That's why they left me: because I'm sensible. Mum's always saying that. That I'm not like Bradley or Perry: I'm better than them. I said if I was better than them I wouldn't be in the same literacy group i.e. bottom and I wouldn't have had to see Dr Khalil all those times when we lived with Carl, but Mum said the hand-washing and the counting stuff is all part of what makes me special and anyway I don't do them any more, do I.

And I don't. Not much.

I'm not in the bottom group for maths, though, I'm in second top, which means I get to sit with Joshua Hillier-Webb, who used to go to Dulwich

Boys before his dad lost his job, and Kelley Eckersley. I wouldn't mind holding hands with Kelley, or even kissing her. Only she goes out with Perry's brother Fergus so I'd probably end up dead, even if she did like me, which I'm pretty sure she doesn't. She did let me borrow her gel pens that time we did budgeting though. Budgeting is so that when you live on your own you know how to have enough money to buy food and pay rent and the hire purchase every month without going to the loan shop. It's easy really, you just have to work out how much you have and how much you need and divide it up. So I've worked out how much food I've got in the cupboards and the fridge and divided it by how many days there are left until Mum and Dean get back. I haven't included the leftover lamb tikka masala though because that's Dean's and I don't like it much anyway. I've got one treat a day, either a Mars bar or crisps, and then it's cereal for breakfast, a piece of fruit and a sandwich for lunch and I can make a proper hot meal for tea. We do Food Technology at school and I can cook five things so far: apple crumble, rock cakes, chicken casserole, cottage pie and home-made pizza. Only we don't have apples, or chicken or mince or flour so it'll have to be something like baked beans or pasta with tomato sauce and cheese. Or maybe I can experiment. Maybe I could come up with something so amazing I could be on TV and end up working in a restaurant like Gordon Ramsay or Jamie Oliver. Dean likes Gordon Ramsay because he once played for Rangers and his cousin in Glasgow supports them, but he doesn't like Jamie Oliver because he pretends to be cockney, which Dean says is an insult, and his tongue's too fat. Dean's not actually a cockney, he's from Kent, but I don't say that.

Something happened. And I don't know if it's Good or Bad. The kind of bad that comes with a capital B.

In the end I made pasta shells with baked beans

and a cheese slice on top. It was all right, though I don't suppose it would be any good on *Masterchef*, but you need proper ingredients for that and we don't have those any more. We did when we lived in Streatham, before Mum met Dean. She was with Carl then and he cooked things with onions and garlic and herbs that were still alive not just in glass jars from down Iceland. Only he's in prison now and we had to move because it was his flat. That's how we ended up here.

But that's not the Good or Bad thing. Making pasta, I mean. It happens when I'm just picking the last bit of melted cheese off the plate and I hear something outside our door. Something that sounds like singing. And I can tell it's not the old guy because the voice is too high, like a girl's, plus it's definitely something like One Direction and I'm pretty sure he doesn't know them. So I look through the peephole in our door but I can't see anything but I can still hear the voice, like really close now. And I have this thought, that what if it's the ghost of a girl who used to live here. Because last year the house four doors down from Bradley burned down because a tumble dryer was on the blink and three people died and one of them was only eight. So I'm imagining how this girl died and wondering, if it was in a fire would the ghost look burnt? And I decide I'll open the door just enough to see but not enough to let a ghost in. Not that I really believe in them, just, you know, like I said, you have all these weird thoughts. Only when I do, something crashes backwards into our flat and it's not a ghost of a girl, it's an actual girl.

I look down at her lying flat on her back on the brown and orange of our carpet. She's about the same age as me, I reckon. Only she's not at our school because she hasn't got enough make-up on and her hair isn't covered in gel, which all the girls' is this term. But she sure talks like them.

"Oh. My. GOD!" She scrambles to her feet, picks up the pile of magazines that are scattered in the doorway.

"Sorry," I say. "I didn't know you were there. I mean, I heard you. But I thought you were ... someone else," I say. Well, I'm not going to tell her I thought she was a ghost, am I.

"I *am* here, innit."

I don't know what to say to that, and then I remember about no one knowing I'm on my own so I go to shut the door but her foot's still half on our carpet and half in the hall so it won't go all the way and she nudges it back open.

"You seen Otis?"

"Who?" I ask.

"Otis? Lives over there?" She nods her head at the flat opposite.

"No."

"He's my grandpa," she says. "Well, sort of. I'm staying with him for a week. I ran away," she adds and stares at me, like she's just thrown a punch and is waiting for me to hit back with something.

But I don't. Because I can't tell her she's crazy to run away because what if her mum's a mad alky or her dad's a — I don't know — a murderer or something. Because then running away would be a good thing, wouldn't it? And I can't trump her because all I've got is Mum and Dean, and I can't tell her about that, can I.

"I haven't seen him for a bit," I say and it's not a lie. I've heard him though, whistling then slamming the door. Going to work, I guess. He's a bus conductor down the Camberwell garage. I've seen his uniform. Dean says it's monkeys' work, wearing the same clothes as everyone else. But I've never seen a monkey in shoes as shiny as Otis's.

"He's probably still on shift," she says. "I'll just wait." And she slumps down against the wall, picks up one of the magazines and flicks a page to some pictures of celebrities in bikinis with red pen rings around bits of them that don't look they're supposed to. No one does look they're supposed to, though. Not round here anyway. Except maybe this girl.

"You still there?" she asks, her eyes not moving off the page.

"Sorry," I mumble and go to shut the door but she stops me again, not with her foot this time but with a question.

"What star sign are you?"

"Um, Aries I think," I say without thinking.

What am I doing? – I actually say that to myself in my head, only I don't seem to be listening. "April the third," I add.

"I'm Leo," she says. "We'd fight but be totally passionate."

I feel heat spread across my cheeks and I'm glad she's not looking.

"Mmgh," I manage.

"It says, 'You're facing pressure in your personal relationships and financial matters. Ordinarily you'd cope with your usual pragmatic side shining through. But with this week's eclipse you're unsure how to handle it all. The answer is to wait for the boat to stop rocking before you decide which way to sail.'"

I'm not on a boat, I think. And I don't have

financial matters. Not unless you count the twenty pounds. Then something flashes into my head — Dean in the bathroom that time, and that plastic bag — and my stomach sort of lurches. But I push the thought away — kind of squish it down into a bit of my brain before I remember anything else. But then I realise I've been standing there saying nothing for like twenty whole seconds which makes me look dumb. And the thing is I want to say something, because I realise I sort of like listening to her talking. Bradley would say that makes me gay, which is pretty stupid if you think about it. But then he is pretty stupid.

"What's yours say?" I blurt out.

"That I'm going to meet a tall dark stranger," she says, but she's not looking at the page any more, she's looking up at me and smiling, and when she does I notice she has a dimple in her cheek, like the hollow in the sofa.

I feel my face redden and my stomach flip again. "Well that counts me out," I say quickly.

"Who said it was you, anyway?" She raises an eyebrow and it feels like a poke in the ribs.

"Whatever ... I don't believe in that crap anyway," I say.

"Yeah, well you should, because last month Charlie Bardwell – she's this girl in my year who once got her thumb stuck up a tap in science – well, her horoscope said she was at a crossroads in her life and had to make a momentous decision and the next week she gets asked out by Flick Everett's brother Jonno and this guy she met down Burger King called Shiv, innit," she says and goes back to the magazine.

I don't want to kiss her after all, I tell myself. Kyle must be round the twist because girls are mental, and they're trouble. That's another thing me and Dean agree on.

Only, if he thinks they're so stupid, how come he always comes back to Mum? And how come she lets him? It's been four times now. Five if you count that night he said he was going, only he went to the Wishing Well and got drunk and forgot. And every time Mum begs him not to leave, then says "Good riddance" when he's gone. And I agree and say "We don't need him" and "We'll be all right, just me and you". Only, when he walks through the door three or four or once thirteen days and seven hours later, she acts like she's won the lottery. Once I tried to run away. Only for five hours, because the library shut after that. But when I went back she didn't even look up from the telly.

"You still there?" the girl asks again after five minutes.

"No," I say. And this time I shut the door and put the chain across.

But all afternoon I hear her singing snatches of songs I recognise off the radio and MTV. Then her sort-of-Grandpa Otis comes back and there's sucking of teeth and he says "Lordy be," and she says "please" a lot, like seven times and he says, "I'll

call her, but I'm not promising anything, child."
And then the door shuts and then it's just me and
the fridge again.

I listen to the hum and then I remember that
house that burnt down because of the tumble dryer
and I wonder if fridges can do the same, and if I
should switch it off, just in case. Then I think
about the ghost again and I decide that even
though it would be pretty sick to see a ghost I'm
glad that girl's not one. And I decide that maybe
she is a Good Thing after all.

Monday 27 May (5 days left)

When I wake up I'm not tired and slow motion any more, I'm awake and buzzing. It's all been lifted off, like when the fog disappears off the Rye in the morning. Then I notice that something else has gone too. And that it wasn't there yesterday either, even when I had to take two paracetamol and drink two pints of Ribena. What I don't have any more when I open my eyes is that sick feeling, that worry that just sits in your stomach, wondering what you might have done wrong today.

You never know what it's going to be. Sometimes it's chipping one of the plates, or getting too many points on Call of Duty, or coughing too loud. Once it was for knowing that the number 36 goes over Vauxhall Bridge not Westminster Bridge. Dean doesn't like it that I know about the buses. He says learning all the numbers and getting excited about which one goes to Pimlico and which one doesn't is the sign of a complete spaz. Bradley says that and all now that he hangs out with Perry, so I don't talk to him about it any more either.

From our window you can see the 12, the 36, the 171, the 343 and the 345 plus all the night buses. I know all of them, even the ones that don't come anywhere near Peckham. But my favourite's the number 12, which goes from Dulwich Library at one end, up Walworth Road, past the Houses of Parliament and Nelson's Column all the way to Oxford Circus. When I was little I thought Oxford Circus was going to be an actual circus with lions and elephants and a high wire and everything and I begged Mum to take me. In the end Carl did and it turns out it's just a massive crossroads with too many cars and people selling roasted nuts. We don't go on the buses any more because I lost the Oyster card and it costs five pounds for a new one plus Dean says buses are for the povvers so we use his Datsun instead. Only one of the seat belts is broken and the gear stick is tied in place with a shoelace and it stinks of cigarettes, which is more povvy than the buses, I reckon.

Sometimes I think I'd like to ask Otis what it's like to be able to go all over London and even out the other side. I wouldn't mind doing that when I'm older: being a bus conductor or a driver. Only you can't say that at school, you have to say Premiership footballer or the army or on TV or you get a right kicking. Plus Dean wouldn't let me.

I wonder then if Nan has a job. One that would mean she wouldn't have been able to come anyway, even if Mum had asked. I expect she does.

She probably works in an ice-cream parlour or in a hairdresser's like Bradley's nan. I realise then that I don't really know anything about her. She sent a postcard once, to the flat where we lived with Carl. Mum went mad though and had a row with him over how come she got the address and then we moved anyway so she's not likely to send another.

I start thinking about the post then. Because Mum'll definitely send a card, with a picture of a beach or Spanish food on it. I bet they're not eating Spanish food though. Dean says it's mostly muck and they're going to go to the English cafés and have fry-ups like here. I don't see the point in that but even Mum says she's not too keen on octopus or pig innards, which is what they have out there. Only, when I get down to the front door, the mat's empty and there's just this pile of pizza leaflets on top of the meter boxes. So I'm wondering if something's happened to the postman – like a fight or something because last year some bloke that Dean knows who's a postman got his jaw broken by someone in Chelsea House because he didn't like the post he was given — when one of the doors opens.

"I thought I hear you."

I turn round and it's Mrs Joyful King. She's in a purple quilted coat, like a sleeping bag with buttons down it and her hair isn't in the right place. I know it's a wig because sometimes it's black and straight and shiny and sometimes it's orange and curling round her face then the next day it's black again. No one dyes their hair that often, not even Shaniqua Green in Year 9.

I want to ask her about the post but then I remember that I need to think about what happens when Dean comes back. I mean, what if she tells him I talked to her? So I don't say anything but I do smile. And it's like she knows what I'm thinking because she says, "No post today. Bank holiday," and I hear her teeth clackety clacking inside her mouth like they don't really belong to her any more than her hair does.

"Oh," I say, without thinking. Then I clamp my own teeth shut so that nothing else sneaks out before I remember to stop it.

"You on holiday?"

I nod.

"Why you don't be down the park with the others?" she clacks.

I shrug.

She looks at me, like she's trying to work out what I'm thinking. And the amazing thing is, she sort of does.

"Not all good them boys, is it. You stay away from them."

I nod again.

"Clever," she says. "Not like my grandson. He mess wit' them bigger boys then they mess wit' him."

I nod then, like I agree. Only I'm really thinking that I never knew she was a nan because I've never seen the grandson that messed with the bigger boys, and what if there's hundreds of nans out there without their grandkids any more, not just mine, and maybe there should be a scheme to match them up or something. Then Mrs Joyful King pulls her quilted coat round her tighter and crosses her arms so that her boobs stick right out. They're massive. Much bigger than Mum's. But then I notice I'm staring so I look down and start to walk back upstairs.

"See you, boy."

But I don't look back, not until I'm up on the second floor and I hear the door slam. And I think I'm alone again, just me.

But I'm wrong.

When I get back to our landing, that girl is sitting outside the door again with the same stack of magazines and a piece of chewing gum she's stretching out so far I think it's going to snap and stick all over her face, but just when you think it's going to go she ravels it back into her mouth and starts chewing again.

"Where've you been?" she asks.

"Nowhere," I answer. It's OK to talk to her, I reckon, because she doesn't live here, so she can't tell Dean.

Only I've said something wrong.

"Like I care, anyway." She pulls the gum out again, winds it round her tongue.

"Why'd you ask then?" I say.

She doesn't say anything then. Just looks at me. Her eyes are narrow, like a cat, I think. Cats watch you like that, thinking stuff. I asked Mum for a cat but she said not in a flat, besides it'd get run over on the High Road. Dean says we can have a dog when we move out, but I'm not so keen on one of them.

I try again. "Your mum didn't drag you back then?"

I heard them last night when I was watching telly. There was banging on the door and a woman's voice, only not like voices round here but more like from the programme I was watching which was set in the old days, like it had all the "h"s and "t"s said properly. Then Otis in his no "h" voice telling her to come inside. Then it went all muffled for a bit so I went back to watching the olden days thing, but really I was wondering what they were saying and if it was like on *EastEnders* maybe, where they talk about big stuff like life and that. We don't talk about life round here, just games and football and what's for tea mostly. Only Dean does the shouting like he's a Mitchell sometimes. No one shouts over at Otis's. All that happens is that the door opens and closes, and then I hear footsteps going downstairs, but only one set so I know she's not gone home after all.

"She said I can stay until school," the girl says. "Otis reckons it'll be good for both of us. She's glad to be rid anyway. She's got work and he's away so it's one less thing for her to do, innit."

I wonder who "he" is. And if her mum lets her say "innit". I bet she doesn't.

I have an idea then. Like a light bulb has just

pinged over my head in a cartoon. I think I could ask her in and we could make sandwiches and play Xbox or watch a film. There's loads of girl films on the DVD shelf. You can tell they're girl films because the boxes are mostly pink and they've all got "love" in the title. Dean won't watch them because they don't have guns or Jason Statham in them but sometimes me and Mum do, when he's gone out. I don't mind them. They might not have guns but they have hope in them and happy endings.

Only then I think about what Perry would say. And the light bulb pings off again and it's back to the dull landing.

"You want a magazine? I've done with some of them."

I look at them in their glossy pile. Mum used to get them. Until Dean told her to pack it in. "They're for girls," I say. "Just pictures of famous people and how to do eye shadow. Waste of money."

41

"That's what you think. You learn loads from magazines."

"Yeah? Like what?"

"Like—"

She can't think of anything. "I knew it," I say, shaking my head. But her eyes narrow again, and she's found what she was looking for in her cat memory.

"Like that you shouldn't do loads of eye make-up and lipstick at the same time, just one or the other otherwise it's like you're a slut."

"Make-up? See, I told you."

She does a funny laugh without opening her mouth; puts one hand on her hip. I try not to look at her chest but she's got a T-shirt on with a pocket right on each boob that kind of pulls your eyes towards them. But then she starts talking again and I'm right back staring into her cat eyes. "And that the Taliban didn't let kids fly kites even or play football, and that there are only a hundred and forty-seven women MPs and five hundred and three men, which is totally unfair, and that you can get cancer from eating too many burgers. That enough for you?"

Her eyes seem wide now, black and shining. Like something has set off inside her and switched on a different part of her. Like what happens to Dean, before he starts shouting words like "useless" and "bitch" and "spaz" and throwing stuff at walls. Only with her it makes good stuff happen not bad.

"I guess," I say, sounding cool, even though my insides are doing something really weird and I can feel my face is hot again.

"Yeah, well. See you."

"No wait," I say quickly.

"What?"

I nod towards her hand. "The magazines. I'll . . . I'll take some. If you're done."

She shrugs, passes me a handful and turns to go back into the flat.

But I'm not done yet. "Joe," I say. "I'm Joe."

She stops, looks back over her shoulder. "I'm Asha," she says.

"Asha," I repeat.

"Yeah," she says. "Don't wear it out." And she smiles, and when she does it crinkles the corners of her mouth and that dimple dips down in her cheek.

Asha, I say in my head, and I smile inside like it's me that won the lottery.

I read the magazines until nearly midnight. I read them while I make a cheese and crisp sandwich for lunch, then I read them all afternoon while I listen to the news on the radio, because Miss Burton is always telling us we should take more notice of the news because it affects all of us, even if the news is happening in China. Only I don't see how their fish crisis or whatever is affecting me, but I'm not going to tell Miss Burton that because she's about the only thing at school I like. Plus it's nice to have the news instead of Absolute 90s, which is what mum listens to, or TalkSPORT, which is the only noise Dean likes.

I read them while I wait for my pasta to cook. And then I read them while I lie in bed with the curtains open and the hiss and grind of the buses braking on the High Road coming in the window.

And Asha's right, I learn loads. I learn that women didn't get to vote in elections until 1928 which is mad if you think about it, i.e. that Dean would be allowed to vote and Mum wouldn't, only he's the one who says politics is all bollocks and hasn't voted ever; I learn that even "safe" sun beds can give you skin cancer, which someone should tell Jeanie because she's always down TanTastic and she's the colour of our front door which means she's probably riddled with the stuff by now; and I learn how to make a meal in minutes from stale bread, tinned tomatoes and black olives. I cut that bit out, even though I know we don't have any olives. But maybe when Mum gets back I can get her to get some.

And I learn other stuff too. Not from in the magazines. But from them just being there, on my bed, in our flat.

I learn that I miss Mum more than I thought I would and that I hope she's having a good time, only not that good so's she doesn't want to come home in five days.

And I learn that I like Asha.

Tuesday 28 May (4 days left)

I shaved my hair off today. Some of it anyway. I saw it in one of Asha's magazines. This boy from a band she likes has a zigzag like a lightning bolt down one side, like Harry Potter has on his forehead. And when I'm looking at it, I think I want one of those, I want to be different because of my lightning hair, not because of all the other stuff.

So I look in the bathroom cupboard to see if Dean has left any of his clippers behind. He shaves off all his hair because of the bald bit on the top, only you're not allowed to say anything about the bald bit, you have to pretend he does it because it looks good. It doesn't. He looks like a thug off the telly. Plus he has a tattoo of a bird, like a swallow or a swift, on his neck. Mum went mental when he had that done and said he'd never get a decent job with a ruddy great tattoo above his shirt collar. Then Dean got mental back and said he didn't want to work for anyone who gave a monkey's fart about what he had on his neck and he'd rather be his own man. Only he's not his own man because he's on Jobseeker's or does stuff for Chinese Tony, when he's not playing Xbox on the sofa. Mum told Jeanie once she thought he was a waste of space. I heard them in the kitchen one night when Dean was down the Wishing Well. I let myself get excited then, let this bit of hope inside, just a sliver, because I thought Jeanie would tell Mum to get rid of him. I like it better when it's just me and her. She's happier then, like there's sunlight in her head instead of damp and fog. Only then she gets too happy and goes out on the town with Jeanie and the next thing you know there's another man moving in, taking up the sofa and selling the Connect Four down the car boot on a Sunday. Jeanie just said at least she's not going out with Gav Arnott because he's been cheating on Bev with someone from down the arcade for six months now so she's lucky if you think about it. I do think about it and I don't think Mum's lucky, not one bit.

I find two sets of clippers – Dean's got three altogether because he got them on a deal from someone in the pub because they'd fallen off the back of a lorry, only they're not actually broken – so I'm in luck. Only the luck doesn't last that long because when I try to do the lightning bolt it just looks like a wave really. And I do it too wide as well. So I don't look like the boy in the band or Harry Potter in the film and definitely not Huck Finn. I just look like Joe Holt only with mental hair.

It'll probably grow back before Mum and Dean get back though. Perry Fletcher has stuff shaved in his head, like an eye, and an arrow and even a Union Jack once, and it always disappears by the end of the week. And if it doesn't I'll just have to wear a hat. I've flushed all the hair away as well and cleaned the clippers so's he can't say it was me just because there's blond hair in there instead of brown. Anyway, maybe he'll come back from Spain a new man. That's what Mum said the time he went to Turkey doing another "little job". Only he didn't come home a new man unless you count the bleached hair and the stomach bug.

But this time might be different.

I made pasta for tea again. With ketchup and frozen peas this time, which is almost like primavera sauce, which Carl made once. It was OK. Only I'd run out of cheese slices because I had the last two in a sandwich with mayonnaise for lunch. And Dean must've eaten the Babybels because I could only find an old shaker of Parmesan so the whole thing tasted a bit like sick and I had to hold my nose for most of it, but at least I'm full now. I'm running out of pasta too. I reckon I've got enough for tea tomorrow then it'll have to be the Super Noodles or the Pot Rice. Mrs Edwards who teaches us food technology doesn't approve of them; she says they're a rip-off and you'd be better off eating the plastic they come in. Mum doesn't like them much either but Dean got a load down the Well for twenty pence a pot because they'd fallen off the back of a lorry and all, so at one point we had fifty of them. There's only three left now. Mum said she was going to throw up if she smelt sweet and sour flavour any more so Dean just ate the rest in the bedroom. He can be nice like that sometimes.

Asha knocks at the door while I'm eating. I know it's her because when I don't answer she says, "Hellooo?" like she knows I'm there and ignoring her, which I am when you think about it. But only because I don't want her to see my hair yet in case she thinks I did it to look like that boy she fancies. It'll be better tomorrow, then I can see her again and I'll tell her I was just out with my mum somewhere, like round Jeanie's or down the bingo.

I'm going to have to go out tomorrow for real though. I looked at the meter and the leccy's getting low so I need to charge the key down Discount Deals. So that means no telly or Xbox for now and then I'm going to ration it properly. Like in the Second World War, only with Grand Theft Auto instead of bacon and butter. There's four days to go, three from tomorrow morning and I've worked out how many units I use a day if I play two hours of Xbox and watch four hours of telly, and if I cut that down to an hour of Xbox and three hours of telly it'll mean there'll be some extra when Mum and Dean get back so they'll be dead pleased with me. I might even get a present.

Wednesday 29 May
(3 days to go)

Asha's gone out. I heard her and Otis leave when I was eating my cereal. Part of me wishes I was going with her. I thought I'd never get bored of being in, what with the TV and the Xbox and no Dean getting in the way of them, but this morning I can't even be bothered to watch *Heir Hunters*, not even to check if my real dad's name is on it and I might have inherited a million pounds. Only I only know his first name which was Terry and that he met Mum on the waltzers at a fair in Newquay thirteen years ago, so chances are I'd get the wrong one anyway.

Plus being in all the time you start to notice all the bad stuff about the flat. Like that our curtains don't even close and one of them has only got three hooks so it just hangs there half on and half off looking kind of sad. Or the crack above the gas fire that keeps getting bigger and bigger. I measure it every month and it's grown two millimetres since January. Dean says it's not worth doing anything about it because you can't polish a turd, but he doesn't even try. He just makes the turd i.e. our flat worse. Like that brown stain next to the window is from where he threw a mug of coffee at me once when I forgot to add the two sugars. Lucky I ducked so it just hit the wall instead and now it looks like a map of India only I don't even say that because Dean doesn't like India.

There's nothing else to look at now. Just the crack and the stain and a West Ham calendar pinned to the back of the door, but even that's two years out of date. We don't have pictures like normal houses, like of sunsets or horses or each other. Not even ones I did at school just put up with Blu-tack like at Bradley's, though he said if his mum doesn't take down the one he did of Optimus Prime soon he's going to pretend the dog ate it because who likes Transformers these days except kids and weirdos? Bradley's house is way better than ours. He's got a plasma screen and a bed that's actually made of wood and stuff not just a mattress on the floor and a computer in his room. Dean says we'll have all of that stuff when we move. He wants us to go to Kent where he's from, to Margate, which is this town by the sea with a funfair and donkeys and fish-and-chip shops on every street. We went there once for a day trip in the Datsun. It was brilliant. Mum and me went in the water while Dean got us 99s off a van on the beach and then we played on the tuppenny falls trying to roll 2ps down a chute to knock other ones off. But Dean got bored and went down the pub and got in a fight with someone he used to go to school with called Sav and then he couldn't drive back because he was drunk and his fingers were all swollen up and we had to sleep in the car.

I wonder if that's why they haven't rung; because Dean's been on the Special Brew again and they've forgot. Or maybe the mobile got lost or doesn't work out there. I checked our phone last night and it's still got a dial noise so it can't be that our one's not working. I checked every half-hour for a bit but then I remembered what Dr Khalil said and I made myself cut it down to an hour then stop altogether because otherwise I'd have to get up in the night to do it. If they'd left a number I could have called them but Mum said it was too much money to call Spain and besides it's better the other way because they don't pay for the mobile calls because it's not really Dean's phone. Maybe that's the problem. Maybe whoever it does belong to has blocked it now so I won't hear anything from them until they're back through the front door on Saturday all laughing and showing off their tans. Maybe I could get a tan if I went out. You can get a tan even in Peckham, and not just from TanTastic. Only then I think what's the point because I'd probably get cancer knowing my luck plus my arms and legs are dead skinny and somebody always calls me Holocaust Boy which is really sick if you think about it, which they don't. Plus what if someone sees me and asks where Mum is. What do I do then?

I think about what we'd be doing now, me and Nan, if she was here. Like maybe she'd take me up West to see a show. Or to the zoo, and I could say, "I'm not eight any more," only secretly I'd love it, because what's not to love about monkeys and lions and stuff? Then I think maybe Mrs Joyful King could take me, and maybe in fact she could marry Otis and then me and Asha would be like cousins or something and we could go everywhere together. Which is when I realise I might have cabin fever which is when you get delirious from being cooped up inside for too long and I decide I really have to go out.

Everything was going to plan, I wore this beanie hat to cover my mental hair and then I think it's like a disguise too, like I'm a fugitive, like Huck when he has to get help from Jackson's Island. And I get pasta and beans and cheese, and ask Ahmed to charge the leccy key and he doesn't even ask about West Ham. And I'm just thinking how genius I am as I go to get the money out of my pocket when I accidentally stand on someone's foot.

"Sorry," I say, and I go to do an apologetic smile. And that was my mistake, because when I turn round, I realise I'm looking straight into the face of Jeanie.

"Joe?"

I could have just run. I could have left the pasta

and the baked beans and the cheese slices and run back out the door and round the corner and down Lyndhurst without stopping until I got to the doorstep. But it's like my feet are stuck to the floor with glue, not just Copydex but superglue, because I can't move anything. Can't even pick up my bag and hold my hand out for my seven pence change.

So I try to figure out what Huck would do, and I reckon I have to pretend nothing is wrong. That I'm supposed to be here, on my own, with a stupid bobble hat on even though it's, like, eighteen degrees outside.

"Hi, Jeanie." I smile, my cheeks stretched and my teeth all out like Mum with her game-show face.

"I thought it was you." She smells sweet, sickly sweet. Of coconuts, like a Bounty bar or the inside of Bradley's dad's car. Better than Lambrini though. She's mad when she's had a drink, like she has too many arms like an octopus and they're always grabbing you and hugging you, or else it's her tongue and she's kissing you like a puppy, all wet and warm on your face. I saw her kiss Dean once when they were supposed to just be having a fag outside the Well. Not on the cheek though. On the lips, for ages, like he's meant to kiss Mum and only Mum. I didn't say anything though, because it wouldn't be a kiss I was getting, not from anyone.

I feel myself lean back a bit in case she tries anything but she's too busy looking at the hat.

"You ill or something?" she asks.

I touch my hand to my head. "No, I just ... I like it," I lie.

Then I see it, one of her octopus hands creeping up, and before I can do anything it's snatched the hat off my hand. And then the laughing starts. She's got a horrible laugh. Not a tinkling sound like Mum's, but this great cawing like a seagull or something.

"What the feck have you done? Has your mum seen that?"

"No," I say, which is the truth, and snatch the hat back and pull it down.

"Dean'll piss himself," she adds.

That's rich, I think, because she's the one who peed herself before. Right on our carpet because she was laughing so much at Mum trying to dance "Gangnam Style" she couldn't hold it in any more. I don't say it though. I just say, "I know" and then I grab my bag and my seven pence and I'm out the door with Jeanie cawing "Joe, Joe" after me on the wind.

When I get through the front door I can hardly breathe and I pray to God and Allah (just in case) that Mrs Joyful King isn't around and all, and one of them is listening because her door is locked and the post is already tidied up. But I should have done a better prayer because when I get to our floor, sitting on the top step with a can of Coke, her back against the banisters and her shiny bare legs stretched across like a roadblock, is Asha.

My heart's already hammering in my chest but I feel it beat harder now. So hard I can hear it pounding blood in my ears; so hard I think she must hear it too. But if she can she doesn't let me know, just swallows another mouthful of Coke and says, "Where've you been?"

"Out," I manage.

"Like, duh."

I go to climb over her legs but she raises one up, stopping me.

"To the shop," I say, thinking that's enough, that that's the magic password like "Open Sesame". But it isn't. Because she's seen the hat, she's fixed on it like a cat when it sees a bird, not letting it out of its sight, like it's going to pounce and nothing is going to stop it. What is it with girls? I think. They notice everything. Bradley would just have said "nice hat" all sarcastic and then talked about the game last night or Dionne Hirst's bum, but not Asha. Because she doesn't just have cat-eyes, she has X-ray ones.

"What are you hiding under there?" she demands.

And then this weird thing happens. It's like someone else is in control of me, like I'm a robot being controlled by an evil overlord, or like Asha's doing it with her superhero X-ray eyes, because instead of kicking her legs out of the way so's I can get past, or pulling the hat down further, I start to peel it off my head. Slowly, centimetre by centimetre, until I feel the last thread leaving my skull in a sort of ping and it's hanging limp in my hand and the stupid wobbly lightning wave is there for her to see, for her amusement. Only she doesn't laugh. She just stands up and reaches her hand out and touches it. And it's like she's stroking a kitten or a puppy, or an ill person, like she can take away the bad stuff with the tips of her fingers.

And I think I must have I known that, and that's why I did it. I knew inside me somewhere that that she wasn't Dean or Jeanie or even Perry, but she was like Mum, who would understand and would try to make it better.

"I saw it in your magazine," I say. "I just thought it would be different."

She doesn't say anything. Just pulls the keys to Otis's flat out of her pocket, opens the door. At first I think maybe she's going to get me something. Like a better hat. But then she looks back over her shoulder and speaks. "Come on then," she says. "If you want me to fix it."

And I do. So I do.

Dean says people like Otis are dirty and live like animals; like pigs or monkeys. But there aren't stains on the wall or holes in the carpet from cigarette butts or a dent in the front door from where one of the Dooleys tried to kick it in once. The flat smells of cake and clean things, and on the walls are velvet pictures of a waterfall and a beach, and on the mantelpieces are pictures of smiling faces: Otis when he was younger with a group of other men all holding up glasses of something; a woman with a hat and a flower on her chest; Asha in a white dress with a woman and a man in Sunday best. Family. A real family.

"Is that your dad?" my mouth says before my brain remembers to stop it.

Asha looks where I'm looking. Snorts. "No," she says. But she's not going to tell me who he is. "Come on," she says again. So again I do.

In the bathroom there are soaps and two kinds of shampoo and a radio that Asha puts on and turns up so we can listen to reggae while she does it.

I lean over the sink and she stands behind me so I can feel her breath against my neck. Each time she runs her hand over it afterwards to make sure it's even. And each time I feel heat inside me. Not the furious rush of a blush or anger, but slow and warm, like syrup again. I don't want it to stop. Not ever. I want to stay here in Otis's bathroom with Bob Marley singing about Three Little Birds and the buzz-buzz of the machine in her hand and the smell of gum on her lips.

But it has to end. Everything ends.

"There," she says. "You can look now."

I bring my head up so it's level with the oval in the cabinet above the sink. And I start, like jerk inside myself, because staring back at me isn't Huck Finn. It's not even Injun Joe. It's someone way worse.

"Dean," I say. "I look like Dean."

"Who's Dean?" she asks.

"My mum's boyfriend," I say.

She pauses for a second. Then makes a sort of snort sound, a half-laugh. "My mum's got one of them."

"Yeah?" I say. Then I think of the picture. The man in his suit.

"Yeah. Right idiot too."

I see myself smile then, see her smile next to my shoulder.

"Is he—" I start to ask, but she doesn't let me finish.

"You don't look like an idiot though."

"No?"

"Not to me."

"What do I look like?"

She stares hard, like she's thinking of someone she knew once, or someone off TV.

She shrugs. "Just Joe," she says finally. "You look like Joe."

"Oh," I say, and even I can hear the disappointment in my voice.

"What?" she says. "That's better than Dean, isn't it?"

And I look, and I see she's right. I look like me. And I am better than Dean.

I just wish Mum knew that.

"You want a drink?" she asks then.

I'm not thirsty, but I don't want to go yet so I say yes anyway. I'd say yes even if it was dishwater, I reckon. But it's not, it's Fanta or Coke so I have Fanta, and biscuits too, cookies with chocolate chunks in.

We sit in the kitchen on these dead high stools, like we're at the bar in the Well or something, Asha's legs dangling so that just the tip of her toe reaches the floor.

"You staring at my legs?" she asks.

I nearly choke on my drink. "No," I say quickly.

She laughs. "It's OK. I don't mind."

Only I do. Because I remember what Dean said so I change the subject. "So how comes Otis is only sort-of your grandpa?" I ask.

Asha's toes kick at the leg of the stool and her fingers tap in rhythm against the tin of the can as she shrugs, as if she doesn't know the answer. And I wonder if her family's as weird as mine is. Like maybe her real grandpa is in prison or Cornwall, or another country.

But he isn't. "My real grandpa died, innit. And Otis married my gran. Only she died too so now there's just him. Only Mum don't like him because he was Grandpa's best friend and she reckons he's a traitor only I think it's dead romantic like it should be a film or something. I might do that one day, make a film of it and I'll be in it too, I can play me."

"That would be sick."

"I know, right?"

And then we're making up this film, and Asha is adding all these characters that I'm pretty sure aren't real, like this devastatingly beautiful blonde woman called Clarissa who tried to steal Otis away only he only had eyes for Betty, who's her gran.

"Can I be in it?" I ask.

"Sure." She grins. "You'll be the boy-next-door who I don't know fancies me and so I go out with this gorgeous and rich but totally evil guy from, like, I don't know, Kensington or something. But then—"

"Who said I fancy you?" I interrupt.

"No one." Asha arches that eyebrow again. "It's your classic film plot though, innit."

"I s'pose." Only I wish it wasn't. I wish it was just about her and me and that she knew what I was thinking right now. "So what happens in the end?" I ask.

"Well, that's the best bit, because this guy cheats on me with this total skank and I am like totally devastated and then you—"

Only I never find out what I do or don't do because the front door opens and slams and then there's Otis in front of us with a massive grin and a Morrison's bag.

"Nice hair, boy," he laughs. "You want to stay for tea?"

I want to. I really want to. But then I remember Dean, and I know what he'd say if he ever found out, which he would, and I slide down from the stool. "Nah, I'd better get back. My mum . . . " I try to think of something, anything he'll believe.

"She welcome too," says Otis.

I've made it worse, I think. And I get that sick feeling again as I realise there's only one way to fix it, and it means more lies.

"She's ill," I say. "Can't leave the flat."

"What wrong with her?" he asks.

"Oh my God, has she got cancer?" Asha blurts. "I read about that in this magazine and this boy totally looked after his mum and like changed her clothes and everything. Like he's looking after her instead of the other way round."

"Not cancer," I say quickly. I think of the magazines, what else did I read about? Then this picture pops into my head: this woman, Mum's age, all weak and pale and lying in bed for weeks on end. "ME," I say. "It's like flu. Only not contagious or anything. She's just tired all the time so she never comes out."

"I see her last week," Otis says.

I clutch at sentences from the article, holding on like it's a lifeboat. "She has good days and bad days," I say.

"Yeah," says Asha. "Like Millie Cartwright's mum has it and some weeks she can get her nails done and have a sauna and stuff at the spa and some days she just watches Sky for, like, hours. Only it's

OK because she has a plasma screen above her bed."

I laugh then at the thought of Mum at the spa or with a telly above her bed only I realise that ME isn't really funny even if it is made up and then I feel sick again for being rude.

"Sorry," I say.

"It's OK, boy." Otis nods. "Sadness make us do strange things."

"See you, then," I say.

"Wouldn't want to be you," says Asha.

"Hey," says Otis and sucks his teeth.

"It's all right, he knows it's a laugh."

And I do and I feel my heart sing and soar that this is something that is just between us. An in-joke. Like friends have. Proper friends.

Or maybe more.

But then, as I'm about to close the door, "Send my wishes to your mum," says Otis.

And, just as quick, the singing stops and my heart is lead and cold as I remember I've told a lie, and a bad one. And how am I going to explain that when she gets back and he asks her how she's feeling now?

And just for a tiny fragment of time, like a millionth of a millionth of a millisecond, I wish she wasn't coming back at all.

Thursday 30 May
(2 days left)

I mixed Cheerios with Coco Pops and Shreddies today. It didn't taste right but I ate it anyway. I wonder what they're having in Spain right now. Probably Full English knowing Dean. In Margate he reckons there's this café that does ten sausages, ten eggs, ten slices of fried bread and a whole packet of bacon just on one plate. If you eat it all you get it free and his mate Fat Dave once did it only he threw it up ten minutes later in a bin on the pier but Dean still reckons it's a victory. I can't work out who won though. Traditional breakfast in Spain is these long sugary doughnuts dipped in chocolate sauce. We learned it in juniors once. I'd try that. I'd try everything. And I'd say *"por favor"* and *"gracias"* instead of "ta". And I wouldn't sit in a pub called the Bulldog watching football all night and drinking lager, I'd go and watch flamenco dancers and guitar players and the men who fight the bulls. Mum should have taken me instead of Dean.

I'm just thinking that and drinking the chocolatey sugary milk out of the bowl when I hear Otis and Asha come out of the flat and shut the door: their feet making two sets of sound down the stairs, Otis's "clomp, clomp" because he's wearing black leather shoes and Asha's "clack, clack" so I know she's got sandals with a heel on again. It's amazing what you can tell about people just by listening. Like now I know that the Polish woman who bangs on the ceiling cries when she listens to old music. And I know that Mrs Joyful

King is a Christian because when she puts her rubbish out in the bins she always sings about Jesus. And I know that sometimes Mr Patel and Mrs Patel fight and one of them throws things and that's when I put my headphones on so's I can't hear any more. I like listening to Asha best anyway. I can hear her humming to the reggae, and laughing with Otis; a tinkly sound, like Mum's, then Otis's all deep like a bear. Then the phone rings and I can tell it's her mum because she only says one word answers and afterwards there's usually a crash sound, like she's kicked the wall or dropped something. Then Otis saying soft words to her before she's laughing again.

I hear her now. I hear the sets of feet have stopped on the second floor and then a "clack-clack, clack-clack" faster and closer, like she's taking the stairs back up two at a time and then there's a knock on my door.

"Joe?" She bangs again, harder. "Joe!"

"Yeah?" I don't open the door, but I'm standing

against it, so close I can hear her hard breath the other side, like the door is just a sheet of tissue paper and I can feel her through its thinness.

"Open up. You gotta come with us."

"Where?"

"The buses. Otis has to work because someone called in sick."

I feel a surge of something inside me, something good, like excitement – the feeling you get at the fair before you get on the Octopus or the Rocket.

"Where on the buses?"

"Nowhere. Just around. We can go for the ride, innit."

Dean would shake his head at that and say she's mental. He'd say I'm mental for even thinking about it, because who wants to ride around in a circle on a dirty bus with the povvers all day?

Me. That's who.

"You wanna check with your mum?" she says as I squeeze through the crack in the doorway. "You know, in case she needs you."

I remember then, what I said last night and I feel the mixed-up cereal in my stomach do this whoosh thing and I have to take this massive breath to keep it all down. I'll tell her, I think; the truth I mean. Just not right now. Right now I need to get out and forget the flat and everything in it and not in it.

"Nah." I shake my head. "She won't mind." And she wouldn't, I think, not if Dean wasn't about, so it's not a lie, not really. But I still feel the cold, hard seed of it inside me. But then Otis is calling up the stairs and Asha's pulling my top and I'm at the fair again, the seed left behind as my heart soars with the possibility of it all, the possibility of London.

It was the number 12. The best. We sit on the top deck, front seats, so we see it all: the drunks on the green at Camberwell dancing to music in their heads; phone shops and shoe racks and fruit stalls up Walworth Road and down East Street market; the Elephant and Castle with the pink plaster

Dumbo and railway arches. Then up on to Westminster Bridge and there, right there, is all London: the Houses of Parliament spreading along the banks like the palace of an evil king; Big Ben telling us it's quarter past ten; and the river snaking through it all, not the silver or blue you imagine, but a wide, brown muddy thing. Asha reckons there's dead bodies down there and lost treasure; that it's full of secrets. Otis reckons all of London's full of secrets, you just have to know where to look.

"You know there's ghost stations, on the Tube. Where they all shut up now, but you can see if you peer out the window?"

"No way! You can see ghosts?"

Otis laughs. "Well, that I don't know, boy. But you can see them old signs. You know once there was a railway just to take dead bodies from Waterloo to the countryside, to this big, ol' graveyard."

"Ugh," Asha and me chorus in union.

"'Necropolis Railway' it called. Railway to the city of the dead. It gone now, but maybe there ghosts down there too."

I like that, Necropolis Railway. A secret train right under people's feet taking away bodies and secrets. It'd make a good film, I reckon, the city of the dead.

"Nah," says Asha. "That'd just be zombies, innit. Zombies on a train, that's like, total boy film. Bo-ring."

Asha's like Otis; she sees stuff everywhere. Not just the bit on the surface, but what's underneath, what's being hidden. After we've been up and down to Camberwell twice we stop looking out the window and concentrate on what's inside instead. We make up stories about the people, where they're going, or what they do. Asha's are the best by miles. Like I'll say, "That man's a banker and he's married and lives on the Grove," or, "She's Polish and works in a shop." But Asha, she has the man down for an international money launderer called Miles Black who's on his way to the basement of the Ritz to meet the head of the crime ring known only as "Slim". And the woman is a double agent working for the CIA and the KGB who's been hunting Slim for ten years for killing her partner Shades. I wish I could see inside Asha's head. I bet it's like one of those junk shops down Lordship Lane: crammed full of stuff. Not rubbish, mind, but incredible things like jewels and rare books and a stuffed monkey in a sailor's hat. I'm not sure about mine. There'd be a lot of numbers, I know that. Numbers make things safe somehow. Because you know where you are with them and they're either right or wrong; there's no weird bit in the middle. Dean's would be black mostly. With a Staffie in it. And a four-pack of Stella.

I wish I knew what was in Mum's head.

I wish something else and all. I wish that days like this with Asha don't end. I don't care that she's a girl. I don't care that she doesn't look like us. I don't care about anything except just knowing her.

So when we're back at the beginning, in Peckham, in our building, on our landing, I squash Dean and Perry Fletcher and all their bad thoughts and retorts down inside me, and from the same place I pull up this piece of courage and I say, "Can I see you tomorrow?"

She has a hand on her hip and cherry gum between her teeth. But she doesn't blow, she pushes it aside and thinks. "What for?" she asks.

"I . . . I don't know," I stammer, the courage popped like a pink bubble. "I like the buses?"

"Otis isn't working tomorrow."

"Oh, OK." I feel my stomach jump and roll, like we've hit the bottom of the roller-coaster ride, and my face goes hot with the shame of it and so I turn away and fumble with my key.

"But we can do something anyway," she says.

And we're flying again, me and Asha up the track to the sky, on a fairground ride of buses. And then it hits me: that I don't want to be in Spain after all. This is where I want to be. Right here in

Peckham in our flat with the stain and the crack and the view of the bins, and the buses and Otis and the railway of the dead.

And most of all, Asha.

Friday 31 May (1 day left)

I hated it here when we moved; hated Peckham and the flat and school and then, when he showed up, Dean. When we had to leave Carl's I begged her, I said, "Can we go to Cornwall, Mum, can we? Can we stay at Nan's?" again and again like I'm some little brat who wants a packet of sweets, even though I don't know what flavour they are. Because for all I knew, Nan could be a wicked witch like in fairy stories. Only somehow, I knew she wasn't. Even though I was only ten I had this feeling that she'd be like a nan on telly, all white hair and flowery dresses, and she'd open up her arms like Mum's the prodigal daughter from the Bible and I'm the son and we'd both run into them and live happy ever after.

Mum just said, "No." Until she got tired of even saying that and just ignored me until I got tired too.

Only now, everything's changed. And even though it's the last day of the holiday today – well, the last day until Mum and Dean get back – it doesn't feel like the end, it feels like the beginning. It feels like Christmas morning used to when I was a kid; waking up early waiting for Mum to get up so's I could open my stocking. Those stopped when I was eleven though because Dean said if I didn't believe in Father Christmas then I wasn't going to get a pile of tat from him.

I'm not waiting for Father Christmas, or even Mum now though. I'm waiting for Asha.

I've been playing Xbox since seven because standing at the door seemed a bit mental and Dr

Khalil said actually games are quite good for someone like me, which really annoyed Mum. Only they're not so good when your hands are so sweaty the controller keeps slipping through your fingers. I ran out of deodorant this morning and all. But I had a shower so I reckon I'll be OK. I wish I knew where we were going though. I hope I'm not supposed to have money because I've only got seventeen pence left.

At least that's the only money I'm supposed to have. Or know about.

And I feel that thing again. That lurch like when Asha told me my horoscope. Or when I lied about Mum.

It's a secret. Like that telltale heart in that story Miss Burton told us at school, where this ba-dum, ba-dum beating sound under the floorboards gives the dead body away. Only this isn't a body and it's not under the floorboards. It's two thousand pounds in twenty-pound and ten-pound notes and it's wrapped in a Morrison's bag and parcel tape and

stuffed in the toilet cistern. I saw Dean check it
once when I got up for a pee in the night, only he
didn't see me because he was drunk and I'm quick.
In the end I peed in a pint glass and tipped it down
the loo the next morning when Dean was gone.
That's when I checked to see what he'd hidden. It's
moving-house money, I reckon, saved up from his
"little jobs". I don't even think Mum knows about
it. And I wish I didn't, too. Because every time I
think about it, picturing all those notes stacked up
and wrapped up in elastic bands, the temptation to
go and check and touch and take is nagging inside
like that little kid saying "go on, go on, go on". So
I think about what Dean would do to me if I did
any of that instead and that shuts it up sharpish.

Maybe she'll want to go to McDonald's. Bradley
says that's what girls always want to do. Go to
Maccy D's and sit with you in the window so's all
their friends and enemies can see. If Asha wants to
do that I'll just say I'm not hungry or something.
I'm not, anyway. I tried to eat the last of the Sugar

Puffs but they got kind of stuck in my throat and I ended up coughing them back up again. Asha would never speak to me again if I did that with a Big Mac.

Asha didn't want to go to McDonald's because she'd got sandwiches that Otis had made. She didn't even want to go up West to look at clothes, which is where Bradley says girls want to go once they've done McDonald's. She just wanted to go to the Rye.

At first I thought she was mental or it was a trick, because the Rye is just this big field with some kids' swings and a slide at the top, only you have to watch where you're walking all the time because of the dog poo.

Asha catches me. She says, "Why are you always looking down? You'll walk into something, innit."

"I dunno," I lie.

"Otis says you'll always be miserable if you look down." She puts on this accent, Jamaican, like Otis.

"You gotta look up, girl, see the glooorious sky." She stretches the word out all long and luxurious, like it's gum, and she laughs and so do I and I do look up and then I see something: a flash of bright green across the cloud. The kind of green that's lime jelly or sherbet. The kind you don't normally see on birds round here who are fat from eating junk and grey with dirt and their feet are all melted away from the acid they put down to keep them off the buildings.

"Oh my God," I say, sounding like someone from one of Asha's magazines. "It's a parrot!"

She gives a little laugh. But not the mean kind. "Nah. Parrots are red and blue. It's a parakeet. There's a whole flock. Look."

And I look really hard, like I'm squinting in the dark of the bathroom watching Dean or down the microscope at school looking at the cells that make up the inside of my cheek. And then they come into focus: tiny flecks of sherbet green in the oak tree. Hundreds of them. Then Asha makes this whooping noise with her hands round her mouth and they all shoot up into the air and swoop in an arc towards the ground, then up again before they land back where they started. I feel something inside me swoop and dive with them. It's a thing of beauty, I think. Like Miss Burton says about books. A thing of wonder. She says that's what books do; they show you that there is wonder everywhere as long as you know where to look.

I just didn't think there'd be any in Peckham.

"How come they're here?" I ask.

"I dunno," she says. "Maybe two escaped from cages and found each other and now there's a whole army of them."

"But this isn't their home," I insist.

"Yeah, well they seem OK to me." She shrugs.

"Yeah," I agree.

Asha goes quiet for a bit then. And I think she's just watching the birds but it's something else she's seeing. Something in her head. "My dad's got another home now," she says. "In Birmingham."

I don't say anything then. Because I'm scared it'll be the wrong thing and she'll shut up again. I just let her talk instead.

"He's got a new wife and two other kids and all. Boys. I never met 'em. He don't want me to and why would I want to anyway? Birmingham's crap, I saw it on telly. All grey concrete and this ugly motorway that goes round and round in loads of circles. Just 'cause it got Harvey Nicks don't make it London."

I think about the parakeets. And her dad. And paradise.

"Better off here," I say.

"Innit," she replies.

We stand there for a bit, taking turns to hoot and watching them soar and fall again. I could stay there all day, I reckon, next to Asha, on this patch of nothing. But she has other ideas.

"Wanna see something else?"

"OK," I say, like it doesn't matter to me one way or the other. Only inside I feel like this is all that matters, being here with Asha. Letting her take me places, show me things. Then I do something crazy, I reach out and try to grab her hand. I love that hand: the dark brown of the backs of her fingers, the pale of her palm, the glint of two gold rings. But she's out of reach before I can get near her. Just as well, really, because I can feel the sweat on me, under my arms, on the soles of my feet, not just from the sun but from being near her. And that's when I realise: she is the fairground ride. Not the bus. Her. And I don't want it to stop; I don't want to get off.

She takes me to see the Ninja Turtles in the old duck pond after that. It's like the park. It just looks ordinary: dirty, with old plastic bags and broken bottles and some slimy rocks. Only when you look closely the rocks come to life, stretching their wrinkled heads out of shells and sculling across the water. Asha says there're dozens in there, because people bought baby ones thinking they were cute like the cartoon, and they got too big for their tanks so they just dumped them in the pond. And even though it isn't the Red Sea or wherever they come from, they've carried on growing and eating fish and are happy.

"Otis says they're like him." She does the accent again. "They just found a way to live, girl."

I laugh again at that, not just because of the accent, but because it makes me happy, the truth of it. I'm not from here – like Otis and the parakeets and the turtles – I don't even know where I am from, not really. But maybe I can be happy. Maybe I can show Mum all this, this wonder, and then we won't need to move to Margate after all. Because this, right here, is paradise. Better than Margate. Better even than Spain. It's like the wide Mississippi in all its glory and I am Huck floating down it in my boat home.

Only then the river washes up something bad. Like a rotten, dead body. Only this one is alive. This one is throwing cherry bombs at the pigeons and spitting on the grass.

"Christ," I say. I feel a swirl in my stomach,

sending everything rolling round like the churn of a washing machine.

"What?" Asha looks round to where I'm staring. "Do you know them?"

"Yeah," I say quietly. "One of them's my friend – used to be anyway. Bradley he's called."

"What about the other one?"

"You don't want to know," I say. Only that is the dumbest thing to say. Because now, of course, she does.

"Who? Come on!"

I feel a trickle of sweat roll down my neck and another down my thigh. If he can't see me, he'll be able to smell me soon. Maybe that's what they mean when they say animals can smell fear. Because I am afraid. I am very afraid. Only I can't tell Asha that, can I. So I copy her and shrug, say his name like it's "whatever".

But it's so not whatever. "It's Perry Fletcher."

He's looking over at us now, nudging Bradley, pointing.

"Come on," I say. "Let's go."

But it's too late, he's got us in his sights like the pigeons and he's not going to let us get away.

"Oi, Holt. Wait."

We keep walking, but I can hear him closing in on us.

"Oi, I said wait."

I don't want to stop. I want to run, in fact, want to fly over this field until I'm a dot in the distance and they're all standing there, even Asha, wondering where I am. Only Asha's not going to let me. She's not even going to leave me here to face them by myself. Because then I feel it, feel the tips of those fingers touching my filthy, greasy palm; feel them snake between mine and grasp, tight, right there and then, in front of Perry and Bradley. And then I stop, not because Perry told me to, but because I know what Asha's telling me. She's saying it's going to be OK. And maybe it is, because I feel like I'm holding a secret talisman or the holy grail or something. I keep looking down

95

to check it's real and it is. I am holding Asha's hand. I can't quite believe it. And nor can Bradley.

"Who's this?" he asks.

I go to speak but she can do that for herself. "Asha," she says. "Not that it's any of your business."

"Wooooo! Got yourself a girlfriend, did you?" Perry looks like he's found the holy grail now, his smirk is so wide.

"Seriously?" Bradley's not smiling. He's stunned, I reckon. Because for all him talking about all the girls he's kissed or touched even over the jumper no one's ever seen him out with a real one. And so I want to say "yes, seriously" but I can't, because I don't know what's going on any more than he does.

But Asha knows. She knows everything. "So what if he has?"

And she didn't even say "yes", but at the second, with those five words, I feel like my heart might actually burst.

"Woooooo! The mentalist got a girlfriend!"

Perry's chanting now; doing some weird dance on the spot like the drunks. Bradley isn't saying anything but he's looking at me like he doesn't know me at all. Like he never knew me.

"Is she as mental in the head as you?" Perry's still going. "She flaming must be."

And then I know Asha is going to say something, but instead the words come out of my mouth, like her thoughts are flying through her fingers and up my arms into my own head. Then I'm speaking, only it doesn't feel like me. It's not Joe Holt. It's another boy who stands up for himself and says what he thinks and doesn't take crap from anybody. "Have you looked at yourself?" says the boy. "Because from here, you're the one who looks mental."

I'm more shocked than Perry, I reckon. But him and Bradley are still pretty stunned. Bradley doesn't say anything, just lets his mouth gape open like he's catching flies. But Perry goes red, and I can feel this energy off him, humming like our fridge only hot instead of cold and getting louder and angrier.

"You are so going to pay for that, Holt."

But even though this other boy in me can see the whites of his eyes and the anger behind them, he isn't scared. This other boy says the one word I've always wanted to say to him. "Whatever," he says, and smiles.

Then Asha is laughing and I feel her pull me and then we are running, both of us flying over the grass and concete until we're dots in the distance, two tiny ants together, one black, one white.

We're sat on the landing, both of us leaning against the banisters, feet stretched out, hands still tangled together.

"He's not lying," I say when I get my breath back. "He'll do me at school."

"So tell your mum," says Asha. "They have to do stuff about bullying now. I read it in a magazine."

"Our school's not like in magazines," I say.

"So? We could talk to her now. I'll be your witness." She squeezes my hand. And then I know I have to tell Asha the truth. Not tomorrow or next week. But right now. Because she told me some of hers. About her dad. And because it's like she's part of me now. And if she's part of me then she has to know everything. Or most of it. Because she'll see it inside me anyway, all lit up and glowing, telling her I'm home alone. And she'll know it when they come back. When Dean writes "the end" all over our story.

I shake my head.

"She too sick?" asks Asha.

I take a deep breath. They always say that in books before someone tells the whole truth. But the thing is it's true, because it's like I'd forgotten to breathe until then and I need all the air I could to push the words out of me in case they try to stick in my throat. "You know I said my mum's got ME."

"Yeah?"

"It's not true."

"What? Is she dead after all?" Asha's brain is on overtime now, her eyes wide. Like this is a film or something. Or *EastEnders*. "Like, there's a body in there?"

"No!" I shout. Then quieter, because she's not the one who did anything wrong, is she. "No. The thing is, she's not here."

"She at work?"

"I wish. She doesn't even have a job, not really. Only sometimes, down the bookies when Jeanie's off. She's . . . " I look at Asha hoping I'm doing the right thing, hoping this isn't going to change what's happening, what I hope's happening. "She's in Spain. With Dean. He's her boyfriend. He's an idiot. He swears all the time and shouts at Mum and he doesn't like foreign people or black people or hardly any people and I don't like him. Anyway they went away without me. They're back tomorrow. But I . . . " I nearly stop then, thinking it's enough, she'll work it out. But something makes me want to say the last bit out loud so that then even I believe it. "I've been on my own. In the flat, I mean."

Asha doesn't say anything. Just stares at me. And I try to imagine what's in her head, like she does with people. I think I can see her say to herself, *That liar Joe, stay away from him*, or *I'm so gonna tell Otis and he'll call the social*. But then she squeezes my hand. "He is an idiot," she says. "If he don't like me."

"Yeah," I say. "He is."

And I know then that she won't tell. And I feel good again. Not that dizzy feeling of flying; not a buzz any more, but a warmth. Like someone has wrapped me in a duvet or inside the fluff of a jacket potato. Like I'm safe. Yeah, that's how I feel: safe. And right then I have that wish again, that Mum and Dean weren't coming back tomorrow. Or I wish just Mum would come back, on her own. That something bad would happen to Dean and it could just be me and her and Otis and Asha for ever.

Only then I have to say sorry even though it wasn't a real prayer and even though I know God's not real because Bradley proved it in Year 7 when he said, "How can God exist if he lets wars and murders and cancer happen." Not even Miss Burton had an answer for that.

"You gonna have to tell Otis some time though, innit," she says. "If we're, you know, gonna stay . . . friends."

My heart jumps and I know right then that if she said "You gotta paint your face blue," I'd do it. "I know," I say. "I will . . . As soon as they're back, I'll tell him."

And right then I mean it. I'll tell Otis the truth and Mum and Dean too. And they won't be able to stop me seeing Asha because Otis is like, like . . . my fairy godfather, I think. Even though Bradley would wet himself at that. But it's true. He can fix anything, I reckon, make it all good. Even with Dean.

*

When I get inside I realise I've left the Xbox on all day so the leccy will probably run out tonight, and I only have pasta with ketchup for tea. Only I don't even feel a tiny piece of worry because it doesn't matter now, none of this matters. Not Perry threatening me or Dean trying to take Mum away or Bradley not being my friend any more.

Because I've got a new friend. And a maybe-one-day girlfriend. I've found my Huck and my Becky Thatcher all in one.

I've found Asha.

Saturday 1 June (0 days left)

I woke up in the night and thought I'd gone deaf and blind or was buried alive because it was so quiet and dark. But it turns out the electricity had gone off. It's amazing how loud real silence is. Like, even when no one's talking or watching telly there was the sound of Dean snoring or Mum getting up in the night to find her cigarettes, then the click-click of the lighter and her sighing. Even with them gone there's still been noise – the rattle and hum of the fridge and the whirr of the Xbox when it gets too hot. But now there's nothing in here. Just my heart thud-thudding and the rustle and swish sound of the duvet on my legs. But then I listen really hard, like I'm trying to hear something above the noise, the silence, and sounds from the outside trickle in; sounds I didn't notice before because all my world was inside these walls. Like the hiss and suck of the N36 on the High Road. Like the cough and complaining of a taxi sat outside Chicago's waiting for girls in too-high heels to stagger out. Like the coo-coo of the pigeons on the sill outside Mrs Joyful King's where she puts out seeds. Like the squawl of cats arguing about which cat is best or who owns which bit of yard.

I listen harder then, to see how far I can stretch, to see if my ears can catch the tick-tock of the clock on Otis's kitchen wall, the rise and fall of Asha breathing as she sleeps. I imagine what she looks like right now, what she's dreaming about. It could be anything – angels or spies or vampires taking over the world. Me, I just dream about football and food and what Perry Fletcher's going to do next.

It'll be different later, I know that. Back to doors slamming and Mum's coughing and Dean's complaining and then his drunk, slobbery "I love you"s. So I clean like crazy. I take out the rubbish and scrub the cooker where the pasta boiled over and even the table where Dean stubbed his cigarette out a week ago and no one had done anything about it. I'm going to show him I'm not useless or mental and I never was. I can't find the remote for the PlayStation but I'll say I never used it, which is true, because who wants to play Tomb Raider any more anyway?

Asha helped me. At first I wasn't going to let her in but she stuck her foot in the door and her hand on her hip and then it's like I'm powerless, that just by moving her arm she drains all my strength.

But the thing is, it feels OK her being here.

Better than OK. Because she doesn't say anything about the crack or the stain or the DVDs that fell off the back of a lorry and are stacked in the corner now. And I know she must have seen them because she sees everything. The stuff that's there and the stuff that isn't.

Like, "Where's your photos?" she says.

"What photos?"

"Exactly."

And she has a point. I mean who doesn't have photos up? Even if they're just stuck to the fridge with a magnet shaped like a banana or a kitten. But we don't. Not out, anyway. But I know where they are – just the two of them. Mum keeps them hidden at the back of her underwear drawer where Dean never looks because it's got women's stuff in it and he says he isn't a poof. I don't see how touching tampons could make you a poof but I don't say that. And it doesn't bother me so I stuff my hand down the back and pull them out.

The first one is me and Mum when I was about

ten. Carl took it and we're smiling big "say cheese" grins at him. Asha says I look like I'm happy and I was. Only three weeks later he was inside and we were back in a crappy B & B in Penge and there weren't any more photos or smiles for a long time.

Anyway, the other one is my favourite. It's of Mum when she was a girl with Nan. Mum's eating this ice lolly that looks like a rocket and Nan is eating a Mr Whippy and it must be in Cornwall because there's no buildings or buses, just green grass, and acres and acres of sky.

Mum said it was perfect. Until she grew up and Nan didn't like her friends or the boys she met down the clubs in Newquay and it turned into a cage. So in the end she ran away with one of them – my dad – back to his home in Bristol, and even though he dumped her after two months for some girl called Sheena she never went back to Cornwall. Mum says Nan visited at first, just a few times. Says she played cards with me for matchsticks instead of money. And Connect Four – before I lost half the pieces. But I don't remember. And then her and mum had a row about Mum's boyfriend – the one before Carl – and that was that except for the postcard that time. Mum's like the parakeets, I think. Run away from paradise and landed up in Peckham. I wonder if they ever think about going home.

Asha said she's going on holiday, only not to Cornwall. To Tenerife with her mum and her mum's boyfriend.

"He's rich," she says. Like it's a dirty word. Like how Dean says "Polish".

I don't get it. "But that's good, isn't it?"

"Not when it's only 'cause he works all the time. She does and all. She's a lawyer. That's where they met. He was on the same case only on the other side. Like if it was a film it would be that they hated each other at first and are always arguing, only in the end he realises she's right all along and she wins the case and his heart."

"Was it like that?" I ask.

"Maybe," she says. "Only in the film they don't show the bit where they've started arguing all over again only this time it's about whose turn it is to take me over Queensway for skating and can't I just get the bus."

I want to hold her hand then. I want to squeeze it tight like she's my real girlfriend not just my in-front-of-Perry one. But I don't. Because she has to go out shopping with Otis so I think about doing it in my head one day and go back to counting down.

Waiting's hard work. I've read all the magazines twice and even done the quiz to find out if I'm a Dancefloor Diva or a Wilting Wallflower. I got mostly "b"s which means I need encouragement to bring me out of my shell. Like a Ninja Turtle, I think.

I want to turn the telly on but I can't, can I.

Our old neighbours Manny and Maya – from

when we lived in this hostel in Earl's Court for a bit – they didn't have one because their mum said it taught them rubbish and limited their imaginations, but there's loads of things I've learned from telly. Like what to do if someone has a heart attack. Or if you get bitten by a redback spider. And how to make the perfect cheese sauce. And how we're all made up of atoms of stardust, which is mad when you think about it.

Plus Bradley watches about five hours every night and he reckons he's going to play midfield for Man U. so his imagination's definitely not limited.

It's four o'clock now and they're still not here.

I thought I heard them on the landing about an hour ago but it turned out to be Asha and Otis coming back from the supermarket. Otis took the bags in and Asha came and sat with me at the top of the stairs like yesterday.

"Have you checked for plane delays?" she says.

"I can't," I say. "No computer."

She thinks for a minute. "You could call the airport. Phones work even when the electricity's off, innit."

"Which airport though? And which flight? I don't even know where in Spain they were."

"Well they haven't crashed," she says finally. "Or it'd be on the news."

"Well that's a bonus," I say, all sarcastic, and she laughs then and it feels lighter, like the tightness around my chest lets go, just for second.

"I wish my mum would go away and never come back," she says then.

"You don't mean that."

"Yeah, I do," she insists. "It's not like she gives a monkey's anyway. Why d'you think I'm still here? Because it's easier for both of us, innit."

"And I thought it was 'cause of me," I joke.

"That and all." She smiles and nudges me with her elbow and I feel that warm, sweet treacle drip into me.

"You'll see tomorrow," she adds. "She won't ask

what I've done or how I am. It'll be about her and Ellis."

"Her boyfriend?"

She nods. And I want to ask about him. Ellis. What he looks like. If he's black or white. If he has hair like Dean or a smile like Otis. Only another word is hanging there in the air all dark and dangerous.

"Tomorrow. You said tomorrow."

"Going home, innit."

And the treacle is gone, just like that. Because I realise I've been so busy thinking about Dean and Mum coming back that I forgot that the holiday is over for her too. That tomorrow she'll be back over the river and out east. Only twenty miles away as the crow flies – as the parakeet flies – but it might as well be two hundred for all the chance of Dean taking me over there in the Datsun or me being allowed to get on the bus.

She nudges me again. "Should we call someone?"

113

"About what?" I ask, thinking there's a chance it's not happening. That with one phone call we could change it all and she won't go after all.

"Duh. Your mum and Dean."

"Oh, that." The pearl of possibility rolls down a crack in the floor. "Like who?"

"I dunno. An aunt or something. Your gran?"

I wish, I think. "Don't have her number. Her and Mum haven't spoken for . . . a bit."

"My mum and Otis were like that, only she worked out she needed him more than she hated him."

"I guess my mum hasn't sussed that yet." I shrug.

"What about Dean then. He must have family."

"Nah." Even if I did know a number I wouldn't call. Dean's family is like Dean, only worse. They live on this estate in a town near Margate. We went there once. It smelled of chips and dog. There were five dogs, all boxers, all chewing stuff and peeing where they liked. Then, when I was eating biscuits and the others were drinking beer, one of the dogs just squatted and did a poo behind the sofa and no one told it to stop or even cleared it up. No one even said anything, like it was just normal.

I don't want to speak to any of them. I could call Jeanie, I guess, but I know what she'd do. She'd get all high-pitched and hysterical and call the police claiming they'd been murdered or kidnapped. She watches a lot of crime series and thinks everything's a conspiracy and everyone is a serial killer.

"I'll be OK," I say. "They'll be back. It's probably just a late flight. The cheap ones are, aren't they? Like at five in the morning or midnight."

"Yeah," she agrees after a while.

We sit there in silence for a few minutes. Not a bad silence, just together but not saying anything. But not even that lasts.

"I got to go. Said I'd help Otis make a cake."

"Sure," I say.

"You could come if you like?"

But I shake my head. Even if Dean is a changed

man he'd still go mental if he found me in a black man's house doing cooking. That's like two crimes in one.

"See you," I say.

"Wouldn't want to be you," she jokes again.

"Me neither," I say and I smile. But it doesn't feel funny. Because it feels a bit true.

I look at the numbers on my old wristwatch, glowing red in the gloom. Eight o'clock. Nine forty-five. Nine fifty-seven.

At 10.17 the phone goes and I nearly jump out of my skin. I'd forgotten it was there even though Asha had said about it. Because it hasn't rung all week. I go to pick up the receiver, but then Dean's voice is in my head saying, "Don't pick up the phone," and Mum's saying except at six, only at six is OK. And I think maybe this is a test, like he's ringing to make sure I do as he told me. So I leave it. I let it ring and ring and ring until it stops and there's just deafening silence again.

116

But as soon as I get used to it, it starts up again. Like the telltale heart it just keeps reminding me it's here. And I think, but what if Dean was wrong, and there is a delay. What if it's him just ringing to say they're going to be late, like tomorrow, and not to worry? Or, better, what if it's Mum saying she's left Dean and can I meet her at the airport or the train station? And if I don't pick up he's going to be even crosser. So I pick up the receiver praying it's not a test, or a robot call trying to sell me something, or Jeanie, drunk down the Well again.

But it's none of them. It's a man, with an Irish accent, and he says, "Is your dad there?" And I say, "You mean Dean?" And he says, "Yeah." And I say, "He's not my dad." And he says, "I don't give a monkey's arse who he is to you, is he flaming there?" And I say, "No." And then he hangs up and so do I.

And I can't decide if I'm glad it wasn't a test or even more scared than before.

*

The last number I remember seeing is 11.58. Two minutes to midnight. It makes me think of Cinderella. That in one hundred and twenty seconds everything is going to go back to how it was. The carriage will turn into a pumpkin and the horses into white mice. And Dean and Mum will walk through the door arguing about whose fault it is they missed the first flight and Asha will go back over the river and I'll just be Joe Holt again. Mental Joe who gets excited at buses and numbers and wears second-hand clothes and once peed his pants in PE.

As I drift into sleep I'm thinking about beginnings and endings again. Because usually the end of a fairy tale is the beginning of something else – of the happy-ever-after bit where Snow White or Cinderella or Beauty marries the Handsome Prince.

But this feels different. This feels like the fairy godmother has been eaten by the wolf and the seven dwarves haven't bothered to come back from work singing "hi-ho" and the magic porridge pot won't stop and is drowning the world and no one even has any syrup.

This feels like the start of something bad. Bad with a capital B.

Sunday 2 June (1 day late)

They didn't come home. Not at midnight and not even at five in the morning.

It's two o'clock in the afternoon now and I'm sat at the window looking down at the bins in case I see them. I haven't so far. So far I've just seen two of the Patel kids, little ones, kicking a ball to each other like they're training for England, one of the students eating a sandwich, and a man leaning against the wall drinking a can of Tango and then dropping it on the concrete instead of in the bin.

He's smoking a cigarette now and looking at the road and then the door of our flats. Asha would probably say he's running a ring of international jewel thieves and he's waiting for Mrs Joyful King to get back from church to send her on her next mission to break into the Tower of London and steal the crown. Only he just looks like a thug in a hat to me. I'm more interested in the sandwich. All I've had to eat today is a cold can of tinned tomatoes and some crackers.

A woman's coming up the path now and I know who she is even though I'm three floors up and the window's blurry.

It's Asha's mum. I know it's her because, even though her skin is darker, she has the same cat's eyes and she walks in the same way: with her head right up like she's saying, *I'm here, world, do your worst.* I wonder what I say when I walk. Then I stop wondering because none of the answers are that good.

The downstairs door buzzes open and I hear her feet coming up the stairs, so I know she's wearing high heels because they clack so loudly on the lino there's a tiny echo. Mum never wears heels. Not even to go out. Says she can't walk when she's had a few anyway so why complicate things.

The door opens before she's even on our landing and even though I don't even look through the peephole, I know it's Otis not Asha who's standing there, waiting. That Asha is still lying on her bed listening to her MP3 player, pulling her gum out long with one hand and tracing circles on the wallpaper with the other. I've seen her do it. It's like she doesn't even notice what's happening because she carries on talking about whatever, but as soon there's a pattern or a line her fingers fly to it and follow it along its course as she goes on about saving whales or being an MP or what Ceri West said to Chloe Newbold in the lower school toilets last week.

The door closes and then it's harder to imagine

what comes next. Like, maybe Asha gets up and her mum hugs her. Or maybe they won't even look at each other let alone touch and Otis is the one doing all the talking, his smile all wide so you can see the gold in his teeth glinting under the strip light. They'll be eating cake soon. Lemon cake. I smelled it yesterday evening when I was counting the swirls on the carpet. Sweet and sharp and hot from the oven. I wanted it so bad my stomach hurt, so I had to eat another cracker. But even they've gone now.

Half an hour's ticked by when I hear the door open again and footsteps on the landing. Not clicky heels or the leather of Otis's shoes, but the soft slide of socks on shiny plastic. Asha.

She doesn't knock. Instead I hear another sound – a soft thud – and I know her head is pressing against the door and she's listening too. To see if I'm in. To see if they're back. I lean my head against hers, so that we're touching through the plywood and glue.

123

She waits until she knows. Then knocks softly, says my name. "Joe?"

"Yes," I say.

She gasps then giggles, because she hadn't expected me to be so close, I reckon.

"You OK?"

"Yeah," I lie. "You?"

"Yeah. I just . . . Otis wondered . . . I wondered if you wanted to come for tea, innit."

And I should say no, because of Dean. But the smell of lemon cake and the feel of Asha is pulling me so hard and so Dean can go do one I think and so I say, "Yes . . . Yes please."

Asha's mum smells like Boots — of perfume and deodorant and cleanness. She's wearing a suit with a white shirt, all smart like she's on *Dragon's Den*. But she looks at me the same way Dean would look at Asha. Funny, isn't it, how everyone's enemies look different. One person's villain is another's hero. Only I'm no one's hero, I think. I'm the baddie.

She sips her tea, sets the flowery cup back down in the saucer. "So where do you go to school, Joe?"

"The Academy," I say. And I see the word hang there in front of me, all spelled right, but the word she reads is different. It says "Failure" or "No-hoper" or something. Like it's a swear word or sour somehow, a word that makes her lips tighten like she's bitten on a whole lemon not just lemon cake.

"I . . . I hear it's improved enormously."

Asha sucks her teeth. I glance at her and she rolls her eyes.

"Yeah," I say. "No one's stabbed anyone for a year."

It wasn't supposed to be funny but Asha laughs and Otis makes a noise like he's trying to keep happiness inside his mouth.

Asha's mum glares at her quickly, then looks back to me and does this crocodile smile, all teeth and no emotion. "So what do your parents do?"

It's like *Mastermind*, I think. Or SATs. All these questions. And I don't know any of the right answers. And I wonder what will happen if I get them wrong.

"My mum used to work at Yates," I say. "You know, the biscuit factory. Now she sometimes fills in for her friend Jeanie down Track and Field. And Dean – he's not my dad – he does ... different things." It's all I can manage. Because I can't tell her about the stuff off the back of the lorry or Chinese Tony or what he's doing in Spain. Even though I don't know exactly what it is, I know it's not the kind of thing you boast about.

"Are they at work now?" she asks.

"Yeah ... No," I correct myself. "Dean's out. Mum's ... " I stumble. Not sure whether I can say it again, what Asha will think after I promised to tell Otis the truth.

But I don't have to find the words. Asha finds them for me. "His mum's ill," she says. "She's in a bed a lot. We made her tea yesterday, didn't we?"

I nod without thinking, like it's Asha making my head go up and down.

"Oh." Asha's mum's smile has gone and it's just teeth and a frown now.

"Oh my God, Mum. She's not contagious or nothing."

"Anything." Asha's mum corrects her.

"Huh?"

"Not contagious or . . . it doesn't matter. Poor you," she adds turning to me now. "So many children are carers now. Asha's lucky."

"Yeah, dead lucky," says Asha, and she give me that look again so's I know she means the opposite.

But Otis sees it and all. "That's enough now, Asha girl."

"Sorry," she mumbles.

"Joe, you take her some cake, when you go," he says to me. "Be a good boy." He stares right at me, into me even. And for a second I think he knows. The way he says "good" like he means "bad". But then he's pouring more lemonade and cutting more cake like the conversation never happened so I reckon I'm OK.

For now.

We say goodbye on the landing.

"Call me," she says. "Or I can call you. He won't be able to tell what I look like on the phone."

Until she says her name.

She sees the thought as if it's spelled out in neon above my head. "I'll say I'm called Anna, innit."

"Yeah," I say. "Cool. Just don't say 'innit'."

I smile and so she does too. "We could have a code," she says. "Like I could ring three times and then hang up, so you'd know it was me. Then Dean wouldn't come into it at all."

"Like in a film."

"Totally." She grins. Then she thinks for minute, reaches her hand out to trace the pattern of my shirt. "He sounds like a right idiot."

"He is," I reply, watching her fingers on the

fabric, feeling the closeness of her. I want to say something, or touch her back.

But she lets her fingers drop. "What are you going to do if . . ." She trails off but we both know what she was going to say.

"I don't know," I say and it's the truth. Because I haven't thought about the "what ifs" of it all. What if they got the day wrong and they don't come back until next Saturday? What am I going to do for food and leccy?

What if they don't come back at all?

"It'll be OK," she says, and her fingers reach out again, but to my face, as if she's going to trace a line on my cheek. But she knows what she's doing this time. Her palm flattens against my skin and she's pulling me towards her and I can smell it – her – bubble gum and lemon cake and toothpaste and she holds me like that. Just for a second, and another, and then it's gone again. But it's enough – enough to know that whatever else happens, this isn't over.

"It'll be OK," she says again.

I nod because right then I believe her. Right then nothing can touch me: not Perry Fletcher or Dean coming back or Mum not coming back.

It's not until I'm back inside – with no food except some tinned custard and leftover lamb curry that's more than a week old; with no telly or Xbox or even light so I can see whether I'm peeing in the right place or on the floor; with nothing and nobody except a plastic bag in a toilet tank that's more than my life's worth to even think about – that I wonder if maybe she's wrong after all.

Monday 3 June (2 days late)

It's school today. Which is sort of good and bad. Bad because of Perry Fletcher. And good because I get free school dinners. Yesterday wasn't so terrible because I had three slices of lemon cake and five Jaffa Cakes and a sausage roll. Otis said, "You eat like you not seen food for days, boy." And Asha said maybe I had a tapeworm because she'd read in a magazine that they can grow inside you and steal your food and you'll be hungry all the time because the worm is getting the toast and spaghetti and stuff not you. I just shrugged and said I was growing.

I miss Asha.

I look in the fridge again in case I've missed something but there's still only the old takeaway and a bottle of brown sauce, plus it's not even cold in there now so I had the tin of custard for breakfast. I'll make it up by having fruit for pudding at school so that way I won't get scurvy, even if Perry Fletcher says only poofs and girls choose an orange instead of chocolate sponge.

My uniform isn't actually clean because no one's been down the launderette and I don't have the four pounds for the machine, but I've scrubbed the mud off the knees of my trousers from football with Bradley on the day Perry was off sick. I wish I could wash it properly though. I wish I could wash me properly and all. There's only so much you can do with cold water. At least there's no PE 'til Thursday and then maybe Perry will be off again so's I can ask Bradley for a lend of his deodorant.

*

I just realized Mum and Dean will be back by then so it doesn't matter anyway because she can get me one down Costcutter. It's weird: I'm so used to them not being here, sometimes I forget they'll be back. Any minute now, even. Like, by the time I get back from school, Dean'll be sat in the hollow of the sofa with his beer and his Call of Duty and his packet of B&H and Mum'll be on the phone to Jeanie telling her about some club they went to and how it was free drinks for a fiver to get in. And then Asha will ring and I can tell her all about their holiday and then I can tell Mum about Asha and she'll invite her round for tea with cake and biscuits and not even the broken kind.

It felt good when I thought that. Even with Dean in the picture. Even though I know what he'd say and what he'd do. Because right now I reckon I could even handle that with Asha around. That's what Mum's DVDs are all about and I never believed it: that love changes everything. Not that I love Asha. I'm just saying that liking someone and being liked back makes you forget the other stuff. That's all.

I messed up. School wasn't even on. It was an INSET day so there was no lessons and no lunch. But that's not the worst bit. I was standing at the gates, sort of peering through in case I was just late or something and they'd locked up because of security ever since Brynn Hughes's dad got into the playground and tried to take him off one break time when I hear this voice behind me.

"You giant knob, Holt."

I don't even need to turn round to know it's him. But I do. Because it's bad enough what he might do to my face but I wouldn't put stabbing me in the back out of the question.

It's not just him either. He's got Bradley and some kid called Skid with him who's in the year above and who's got his name tattooed on his knuckles. Bradley used to say it's so's he doesn't forget 'cause he's so stupid. Only he's not saying that any more, I reckon. And now it's three against one, even if Bradley is looking at his shoes like there's something totally fascinating on them.

"Your mum too drunk to remember when school starts?"

Bog off, Perry, I think. But what I say is, "No."

"Or do you fancy Bloater so bad you just can't live without him for one more day?"

Skid laughs at this, like it's the funniest joke in the world, and Bradley looks up from his shoe and does a sort of snorty sound to show he's with them after all.

Bloater – Mr Goater – is our deputy head and he's dead huge and wears elastic trousers and everyone, not just Perry, reckons he's gay just because he sings in this male choir. I don't mind him, really, but I don't tell Perry that or he'd tell the whole school I was doing him for sure.

Instead I try to think what he'd say, if he were me. "I just messed up, all right," I say. "You know how it is."

But I'm an idiot. Because Perry would never be me, not in a million. He doesn't show up to school half the time anyway so he's hardly likely to turn up on the one day it's not even open. I know it, and he knows it. So we're staring at each other – me, Perry, Skid and Bradley – all of us waiting to see what Perry's next move is.

"You owe me a quid," he says.

"What for?" I ask, like the idiot I am.

"So I don't tell anyone about you and your . . . girlfriend."

"What about her?" I say. Before I remember that she isn't. Not really.

"That she's only with you 'cause she feels sorry for you 'cause your dick don't work."

I feel my face redden. "It does," I say quietly. I think.

But that's not the point.

"So give me a quid, every day, and that's exactly what people will think. And I won't have to kick the crap out of you neither."

"I can't," I whine. But it's hollow, pointless, because we all know he's won. And that if I don't my life is over, as if it wasn't pretty messed up already.

"Tomorrow, after school, behind Chicken Hut."

And then he's off down the High Road like a villain with his henchmen. One of them – Bradley – looks back. And for a second I think he's going to pull a face; one that says, "Sorry, mate" or "I'll make it OK". But his face says nothing and he just turns back and keeps on walking.

I don't blame Bradley, not really, because you're supposed to keep your friends close but your enemies closer – I learned that off the TV and all. But he's not keeping me close any more. So I'm not a friend or an enemy. I'm nobody now.

I sit in the library for a bit, because it's warm in there and the lights are on and I can read the papers and magazines. But I realise I don't care that there's a war in Syria or that Jennifer Aniston might be getting married or that somewhere in some other country something bad is happening. All I care about is that Perry Fletcher is going to tell everyone about me and Asha and say I can't even get it up and probably beat me up while he's about it unless I get a pound by tomorrow and the only chance of that happening is if Mum and Dean are back at the flat by the time I get there.

But that kind of thing only happens in films and on *EastEnders* and *Coronation Street*. Real life never works out like that. So when I get back there's no Mum coming up the road with the shopping bags, or Dean heading down the Well with a fag on the go.

But someone's there. Leaning on the wall outside the flats, smoking a cigarette and playing Angry Birds on her phone.

Jeanie. She's been down TanTastic and had her hair done so she looks like a kind of a tangerine with a wig on. I don't get that. Why would anyone want to look like that? Or kiss a woman who looks like that? That Dooley must do though and you don't want to argue with him any more than you want to double-cross Perry Fletcher.

Part of me wants to carry on walking. But most of me knows there's no point because even though she hasn't looked up from the game, she knows I'm there.

"Joe," she says, her fag hanging off her bottom lip like it's stuck on with superglue not lipgloss. "Hang on . . . Hang on . . . " She presses buttons frantically and then lets out this massive sigh, like she's just run the marathon or something, not catapulted stuff at pigs that don't even exist.

She finally looks up. "Joe," she says again. Then, "Joe-Joe, come on, give your Auntie Jeanie a hug."

I should hate that name – a baby name – but it's what Mum used to call me too. So I let her put her skinny arms around me. She smells of smoke and too much perfume. And I'm pretty sure there's ash falling down my back.

"What you doing all dressed up like that?" she asks pulling back and looking at me properly.

"I forgot it was an INSET day," I say. Then add, quickly, "Mum forgot."

"Christ, she'd forget her own arse if it wasn't attached," she laughs.

"Yeah," I sort of laugh back. Even though it's not funny and not even possible.

"So where is she then?" she asks.

I feel my legs go weird. Like they're not there for a second and I have to put my hand against the wall to steady myself. Because I don't even know if Jeanie knows she was away. And I really don't know if I can say she never came back.

"Out," I manage.

"Dean with her?"

I nod. Because he probably is. Like a bad smell, Mum joked once, always hanging around. But this isn't funny either. Because he never lets her go anywhere on her own. Not unless it's the shops to get him cans or fags or lottery tickets. Once, in a club, he went to the toilet with her. I heard her tell Jeanie. But that was Jeanie's fault because she'd got off with Greg Stanton in the loos at Chicago's when her actual boyfriend was on the dance floor doing the Macarena.

"I been trying to ring her for days. How come her phone's off?" she asks. "That Dean again?"

"Nah," I say. "Just run out, I think."

"Typical," she says.

But it's not. Even if it were true, Mum never used to do stuff like that: forget to pay the bills. Or not have the money to pay them. Not in the old days. Not with Carl, or Jonny before that, or whoever before that. Or when it was just us. She can do all the stuff she needs on her own. Just that she's forgotten she can. And Dean doesn't bother to remind her. Tells her she'd be nothing without him so now she believes him.

"Tell her to pop round then, will ya? Dean too. Mickey wants to see him."

Mickey. That's the Dooley she's seeing. I nod. "I

will," I say. *When I see her*, I add in my head. Whenever that is. This week, next week, some time, never. And I try to sound cool about it, even just to myself. Because it's like Dr Khalil said, if I tell myself to be cool about it I can be.

Only I caught myself counting the woodchips on my bedroom wallpaper this morning, which isn't cool at all.

The phone doesn't ring at all. Not Asha's three rings, or more from Dean and Mum, or the endless ones from that man. I wish I'd taken Asha's number now, wish I could call her just so's I could hear her voice all honey and "innit", telling me what she's done, who she's seen. That'd make it all right, I know it would. I could ask Otis, I think. But the less I see of him the better, at least until Mum gets back. Plus Dean doesn't like me using the phone anyway because it costs too much.

There's really no food now. Only the takeaway and a packet of old hamster pellets and I tried one of them and I couldn't even swallow it. What's the point of teaching you about budgeting at school if they don't tell you what to do when the money runs out? What happens then? That would be a better lesson.

In the end I eat the lamb thing. Dean says curry was invented to disguise old meat anyway because that's all they can afford in India and the spices kill the germs and cover up the bad taste. And it works because it doesn't taste any worse than it does when it's new or hot. I don't know what I'll do tomorrow though.

Tuesday 4 June (3 days late)

I feel like I'm dead.

But I'm not.

I wish I was though.

Do I mean that?

Yes, I do.

I've been sick seventeen times now and I lost count of the other end.

Dean was wrong. I should have known it. He gets sick every time they go down The Raj and he says it's just a dodgy pint but it's probably the lamb after all. And that's when it's new, not a week old.

I should call in sick to school but every time I try to pick up the phone I have to throw up again. What's the worst they can do anyway? Send a note home? There's no one to read it.

Asha called. The phone rang three times and stopped and then started again, but I was still in the loo and so I couldn't even get to it in time. Then an hour later I heard the ringing and I was about to grab it but that time it didn't stop after three so I knew it wasn't her so I just looked at it, willing it to shut up and leave me alone. I know who it was. It's that Irish guy, the one who wants to talk to Dean. A Dooley, I reckon. Jeanie's Dooley. She said that he wants to see Dean. It'll be about a job, maybe the one in Spain.

But then I remember Jeanie doesn't even know they went to Spain and I think maybe the Dooley doesn't either and that's what he's mad about.

*

I've run out of loo roll now. And I've looked for kitchen roll or even magazines but I remember Asha took them all with her and so there's nothing. When we were in the hostel we used to borrow stuff off the others all the time and they'd borrow off us – sugar and milk and fags and stuff. Except the only one I can borrow off here is Otis. I weigh it up – the chances of him asking about Mum versus me needing loo roll and I'm feeling queasy again already so I decide I'm just going to ask him and say I don't have time to talk, not today. Not yet.

Only Otis always has time.

"You look terrible, boy," he says.

"I know," I reply. Don't need to look in the mirror to know what I must look like – all sickly and yellow and the shaved head won't help.

"That man not here to look after you?"

He means Dean. I shake my head.

"What about family?"

146

"My nan lives in Cornwall," I tell him. I just don't say the rest of it.

"It not right," he says, like to himself now. "Family all spread far apart. You need help, you and your mother."

"He'll be back soon," I protest. "Dean, I mean."

"Really?"

I look at him, and I want to tell him so bad, I want to tell him there's no one and for him to hug me like he's my sort-of-Grandpa not just Asha's and to take me in and make me chicken soup that will cure me and wash my clothes and let me lie in a hot bath with bubbles 'til all the sour smell and the sickness is washed off me. But instead I just say, "Really."

He stares at me hard as he hands me a loo roll, like he's trying to see in my head to work out what's truth and what's lies, only even I don't know any more I've told so many.

"That all, boy?" he asks.

"Yes . . . No," I say, remembering. "Asha – can

you tell her I'm sorry I didn't answer the phone. Can you ask her to call me tomorrow?"

"You can't call her?"

I shake my head again. I could if I got her number. But Dean would know – it would be on the bill. Then I'd be for it.

"OK. I tell her."

I mumble thanks and I'm just about to turn when he says something else. "You know I'm on your side, boy."

And I look at him. And I believe him. And I nod and then he closes his door, and I close mine.

And as I lie in bed that night when there's nothing left to come out of me, I realise him and Asha – they're the only ones now. The only people on my side. Not Dean, that's for sure. Not even Mum. Because it's her fault this is happening, all of it. And so I hate her. I hate her, I hate her, I hate her. And I hope she isn't ever coming back.

But I wish she was here.

And I turn on my side to face where I know the wall is in the darkness, and with my big finger I start counting the woodchips in threes.

Wednesday 5 June
(4 days late)

I feel hollow inside. Like an Easter egg or a rotten conker. Like there's nothing to me but skin and hair and the clothes I'm standing in. It's as if I've got rid of it all: not just the food but the anger too. All the feeling. It's like I'm numb. I'm numb when I get up and try to shampoo the sick out of my hair with washing-up liquid. I'm numb when I pull my uniform back on even though it's creased and there's a stain down one trouser leg. I'm numb when I walk down the stairs and out the door and

on to the High Road. And I'm still numb when I
sit down in registration and say "Yes, miss," when
my name is called and "Sorry, miss," when she asks
how come no one let her know I was off yesterday.
Nothing sinks in, nothing touches me inside.
Nothing makes me happy or sad. Not when we do
Africa in geography and I know that the capital of
Kenya is Nairobi. Not when I hear Bradley tell
people he kissed some girl called Katy down the
lido and she had boobs bigger than Miss Mynott.
Not when lunch is spaghetti bolognese and I eat all
of it, even the carrot chunks, which aren't even
supposed to be in it according to the telly, because
I'm so hungry. Not even when I'm standing round
the back of Chicken Hut after school waiting for
Perry 'cause I figure if I don't show he'll only make
it worse.

I thought about taking it. The money, I mean,
from Dean's stash. I stared at the toilet for a
whole hour this morning. Thought about
reaching into the cistern and pulling up the bag,

unwrapping it from the wetness and taking out a single tenner. One wouldn't be missed, I thought. Only one.

But then the other thoughts started. The "what ifs". What if I took twenty? Then I could buy a pizza from Pizza Hut for dinner as well. What if I took a hundred pounds? I could get new trainers like Bradley's. What if I took it all? What could I buy with two thousand pounds? I could get two hundred pairs of trainers. Or two thousand scratch cards. Or four thousand packets of Tic Tacs, only no one would do that, not unless they were mental, and that's when I knew I had to stop staring and stop thinking about it because I couldn't take just one note. Because I am mental.

I'm Mental Joe. I'm a robot now. I just do what the buttons tell me.

"So where was you yesterday?"

"Ill."

"So you better have it now, then."

"I haven't got it."

"Are you flipping serious?"

"Yes."

"You're in shit, Holt. Big shit. That's three quid you owe me tomorrow."

"I know."

"You better have it then."

"OK."

"It's your last chance, Holt. I mean it."

"I know."

It's not 'til I'm back at home, in a sick-stinking flat, sat in the hollow made by Dean's backside on a sofa where Mum used to put her arm round me when we watched *Doctor Who* in case I was scared, which I wasn't, but I let her anyway, that I start to cry.

I cry so hard I think I might choke because not just tears come out but snot too, great threads of it like snail or slug trails hanging from my nose and sliding on my cheeks. I cry so hard it makes my whole body judder and shake, like I'm having an epileptic fit or something. I cry so hard that there's a bang on the floor from the sad Polish woman telling me to shut up because she's trying to watch *Deal or No Deal*.

So I stop then. The noise anyway. Because my body is still shaking when I hear the end of the programme downstairs, and it's still shaking an hour later when the phone rings and before I can even check what time it is or wonder whether it's a good idea or not my arm reaches out to pick it up.

"Hello?" I say. And I can hear how scared I am then. Like it might be the police or the social services or Mickey Dooley – my Injun Joe – calling to say they're coming to take me away.

"Joe?"

I let out a noise then. Like a strangled gasp or a gurgle. It's not the baddies. It's not even Jeanie. It's . . .

"Asha, innit. You all right."

"No . . . Yeah. Kind of. I was ill."

"I know, Otis called. You're OK now though?" She sounds like Mum. Proper concerned, not like Dean who's just hoping he won't have to actually do anything, or the teachers who don't want you to give whatever it is you had to them.

"Yeah. I ate some dodgy lamb."

"Blimey, lamb. Your school's nicer than mine. We only had pasta."

I don't say anything to that. Because if I tell her the truth she'll know I'm mental. And anyway, there's a worse truth I have to confess.

"So they come back then?"

I feel another surge of sickness but it's nothing to do with what I've eaten. It's about what I have to say. I have to tell her because no one else knows and no one else can understand. "No," I say finally. "They never came home."

"Oh my god," she says. And then she's silent for a bit. Then "Oh my god," again.

"I know."

"Bloody hell, Joe. What're you going to do?"

155

"I dunno," I say. Because I don't. I don't have a Plan B. Didn't even have a Plan A other than watching how much I ate and how much leccy I used and look how bad that one worked out.

"I can come over on Saturday," she says. "Mum's got a conference and she's gonna ask Ronnie Green's mum but I'll say I got to go to Otis's instead. All right?"

"Yeah," I say. And I mean it. Because it will be, once she's here. Because even if Mum and Dean have decided to stay another week, if I can just wait until the weekend, everything will be all right. She'll know what to do. Her and Otis. They'll fix it.

"You wanna hear what happened at school today?"

And I smile then. For the first time since Sunday I actually smile. And the smile stays while I let her tell me about this girl and that girl and who fancies whose brother and who got a love bite off a waiter in Crete. And I say stuff like "no way" and "wicked" and "sick" and I even laugh. Because when she's there, at the end of the phone, it's like I can feel her goodness shining around me and lighting up the room, so bright I can't see any of the crap that's there or the stuff that should be but isn't. I feel like I'm floating on it, like I'm swimming in syrup now, her treacle voice carrying me on a wave.

"My mum's calling me. I got to go, innit."

And the wave hits the rocks and me with it.

"OK," I say. Then, "Saturday, yeah." Forgetting what Bradley told me, that to get the girls you have to play it cool, make like you hate them, then they'll come begging for it. Instead I do the opposite; act like I'm desperate. Because I am.

"Yeah, Saturday."

"Brilliant!" I blurt. Then try to pull myself back from social suicide. "I mean, sweet."

She laughs but I think it's with me, not at me. And that's OK.

"See you," she says.

"Wouldn't want to be you," I reply quickly.

"Liar," she says.

"Whatever," I throw back.

She laughs again.

Then I hear a voice in the background. "Asha? Asha!"

"I really got to go now. Bye."

"Yeah, bye."

And I hear the clatter of the phone being dropped into the handset and then she's gone and I'm back in the real world with no warmth and no light and just the dull monotone of the dial sound instead of the up and down, the music of her voice.

It's still early but I crawl into bed. Because the phone isn't going to ring again. Because there's nothing to do. Because I'm tired out from the crying. Because the flat is cold now and my duvet is warm, even if it does smell bad. Because the quicker I get to sleep, the quicker it'll be tomorrow, and then the next day, and then the day after that is Saturday and Asha will be here, not just at the end of the phone but right here, in this room with her gum in her mouth and her hand on her hip and her fingers on me.

I jerk awake to the sound of our door buzzer. I know it's not morning yet because I can't hear enough traffic outside and in fact it's not even night, not proper because I can't hear a thump thump of drum and bass from Chicago's so it mustn't even be eleven yet.

The buzzer goes again. A horrible sound, like a poke or a sting. Jabbing at you, willing you to move, saying "get up, get up, get up".

Jeanie, I think. It's Jeanie, drunk and she hasn't got the cab fare home and she wants to kip on the sofa. Mum lets her in like that at least once a month. But I can't. Because she'll know as soon as she walks in the door.

It buzzes a third time, long and loud, someone's finger pressed against it and they're not letting go. *Shut up*, I think. *Shut up, shut up, shut up or you'll wake Mrs Joyful King and the students and the sad Polish woman and the Patels.*

And, worse, Otis.

But I still don't move.

Then I hear it. Hear him.

"Oi, Lister. I know you're in there."

You know nothing, I think, 'cause Lister's Dean's surname and he's miles away.

"Come out and bring it with you."

What's "it"? I think. But then that picture comes into my head – the telltale heart. Dean hunched over the toilet cistern, a plastic parcel in his hand. Then me on the floor, counting the piles, rewrapping it, putting it back. He's after the money, I think, and I feel sick rising in me again and have to swallow it down. The money's not Dean's at all. It's his – Mickey Dooley or one of his henchmen or whoever it is. Then I remember the man who was lurking outside the other day who dropped the Tango can on the concrete. That's who this voice belongs to. Not the slick head of an international criminal ring like Asha reckoned. But just another greedy, angry thug from down the Well. She doesn't see it all, I think. Not the stuff she doesn't want to.

The buzzer goes on and off and on and off, fast and loud as my heartbeat. "Come out or I'll come in. You fecking know I will."

But I couldn't move even if I wanted to. Because what would happen? He'd take it out on me, take the money, and then where would I be?

Dead, that's what. Or as good as.

So I lie there like a corpse while he shouts and raves. I lie there until one of the students finally tells him to "eff off" and unbelievably he does but not after calling them a word that I never even heard Dean use. I lie there until eleven o'clock, twelve o'clock, one o'clock counting the seconds in my head, saying them over and over, as well as sorry to Dr Khalil and to Mum, until at some point I can't even remember how to count any more and sleep takes me.

But I wish it had been something else. Something longer. Something where I wouldn't wake up to this room or this flat or this stupid broken-biscuit, stain-on-the-walls, cracked-open life ever again.

Thursday 6 June (5 days late)

But I do wake up. Because that's how it works isn't it. Life's not like it is in stories or films. You don't get a genie in a lamp and three wishes or a magic ring or a wardrobe with a whole other world behind it.

But I do get what's coming to me.

I'm late out of school because Miss Burton is hassling me about a note I haven't got signed about some trip to see some Shakespeare play. I tell her it's pointless even sending it home again because it's a tenner to go and we don't have it and even if we did Dean would say it's for poofs and girls and I can just read the bloody book if I have to. Miss Burton sighs when I say that, like she's heard it before. Which she probably has round here.

"Just get it signed and I'll see what I can do," she says. Like she can wave some magic wand and conjure money from thin air.

I wish she could. I wish I could. But I can't and I haven't and now I've got to go and tell Perry Fletcher that.

"All right," I say and I'm pretty sure even she knows it's a lie but I'll forge the signature myself. I've done it before enough when Mum really was ill that time and couldn't get up in the mornings. Or evenings. And once when she'd broken her fingers. It doesn't even feel like cheating because everyone does it and the teachers know it.

"Tomorrow," she says.

"Tomorrow," I repeat.

Tomorrow never comes, I think.

But it did yesterday, because it's today now and there he is, on his own again, leaning against the industrial bin, smoking a cigarette and kicking at a crumbling brick.

"So you got it?"

I don't even bother to put up a fight. It's easier that way.

"No," I say.

"Well, you knew what would happen." Like he's a teacher or a dad telling a kid off. Only dads round here don't talk much like that. They do it another way. This way.

I nod.

And then it starts.

I see a blur of blazered arm then feel his fist hit my temple, the knuckles digging in above my brow bone. It doesn't ache like I thought it would but stings, like my face has been flicked by a giant, so that my brain inside wobbles and sends blood and sound resonating out to every cell and a burst of white stars scatter from the corner of my eye. I think I'm going to throw up again, but I don't.

The second punch ricochets off my cheek and cracks into my nose. I feel it shift upwards but I don't think it's broken. Doesn't stop the blinding pain though. Doesn't stop it bleeding though. A slow, thin trickle that drips into my gaping mouth so I can taste the metal of railings or copper coins.

The third one floors me. My legs give way and I slump against the bin, sliding down the scratched blue plastic into a heap of brown lettuce and half-eaten chicken wings and empty ketchup cartons that stick to my hands. When I was a kid I thought blood looked like ketchup. Even in Year 7 me and Bradley used to squirt it on our tea and pretend we were murdering it. But now, side by side, I see how different they are. One is a bright happy colour – proper red, like lipstick or balloons. The other is dark, brown almost. And thin, mean, like ink.

Not the same at all.

"It's a fiver tomorrow. Or it'll be your balls next

time. So's you can tell your girlfriend they don't work along with your dick."

My hands go to my crotch without thinking. Fletcher laughs, then spits a thick, white gob of phlegm that sticks to my shoulder.

I don't even flinch. Not because I'm not scared or disgusted, which I am. But because I can't. There's no point, after all, is there. I'm just Joe. Mental Joe. And he can do what he likes, just like Dean, and just like the others before him.

So I just wait. For him to go. And for the noise in my ears and the pounding in my head to stop, and my one good eye to open enough to see where I am, and my legs and arms to work well enough to haul me up against the bin, wipe the worst of the blood from my face, and then walk me slowly back out into the street and down the High Road home.

I'm expecting the shouting man to be there again, waiting for Dean. Because that's the kind of stupid soap opera storyline that would just happen to me. But there's no one out, not even Mrs Joyful King pointlessly watering the one pot plant that the dogs will only pee on anyway.

But when I get to the top of the stairs I realise why the coast was clear down there. It's because the storywriters have got someone else in mind.

Otis.

He's coming out the door with a bag in his hand. Going to Morrison's or Discount Deals, I reckon, for milk and biscuits or maybe a can of Guinness. But he stops when he sees me and I don't need a mirror to know what I look like because it's all over his face too. It's bad. Worse than I thought. Not something I can just stick a plaster on and no one will know any different tomorrow.

"Come with me, boy," he says. And I don't even bother to try to hear what Dean would say, I just follow him in, let him close the door behind me, then lead me back into the bathroom where Asha shaved my head.

I was right. It's bad. My left eye is closed and the lid is purple and bulging out, like it's a hard-boiled egg under there not an eyeball. My nose is swollen and there's blood smeared all over my face and down my shirt. I think it's a wonder no one stopped me, tried to take me to hospital. But then they don't, do they. Because I probably deserved it. Or I might do it to them. So they leave well alone. That's what Dean says, stay out of it or you'll end up in it up to your ears and if it's shit, you won't like the taste of that.

But Otis hasn't heard that or doesn't care. He runs the hot tap, gets out bottles of witch hazel and TCP and some cotton wool, then he gets to work.

He's like Asha, I think. Not girly, obviously, and his fingers aren't as quick, and he doesn't smell of gum. But he's slow and soft and he hums while he's doing it. That song from the radio about the Three Little Birds saying everything's going to be all right.

I wish the song was true.

"You hungry?" he says when he's done, when I'm sat on his flowery sofa with a cup of tea so sweet and milky it makes my teeth feel funny.

I nod. Of course I am.

He gives me chicken with "rice and peas", which turn out not to be peas at all, like Dean reckons, they're kidney beans, so it just shows how much he knows. As I eat he asks me stuff. Easy stuff at first.

"Boy at school done this?"

I nod. *Yes.*

"It gonna happen again?"

Shrug. *I don't know.*

"Your mum know?"

I shake my head. *No.*

Then the questions change. And the baddie Otis is coming out. The one hidden under the gold teeth and the smiling eyes and the singing.

"Where your mum?"

I don't say anything. Don't nod or shrug or shake my head.

"I don't be seeing her for days now, boy and I know she not ill."

Nothing.

"She gone?"

Nothing.

"You can tell me. You can tell Otis."

I shake my head then. Because I can't, can I? Because I know he says he's on my side but if I tell him he'd have to call the police because that's the law, and he's not like Dean, the law means something to him. And because I'm not sixteen the police will call social services and then they'll come round and get me and I'll go in care like the O'Connell brothers and they reckon it's not like on *Tracy Beaker* at all. It's all damp rooms and fighting and different foster parents every month and that's if you're lucky. If you're not you go to Wardley House and then you might as well be in prison.

So even though part of me wants to blurt it out like I blurted to Asha, wants to spill the secret that's all tight and hard and hurting inside me, I know that as soon as it's gone something worse will take its place. And so I don't. I say, "I got to go," and stand quickly so my chair scrapes along the shiny wood of the floor and clatters against the wall.

Otis looks at me long and hard like he's sizing me up, working me out, weighing me to see if I'm a good egg or a bad one.

"Asha know about your mum?"

I nod.

"She a good girl; loyal. But she a girl, you get me? A chile. She don't always know what best."

"But—"

"You need someone, boy. You need your granny. Life too short and hard for differences. Me and Chrissie we learn that the hard way."

He means Asha's mum I think, remembering her crocodile smile. Chrissie – the name doesn't fit somehow. Chrissie sounds fun and easy and she's all tight and cross. But then I think of mum's name – Emily – and I don't reckon that fits how she turned out either.

"I have to go. Please," I beg, even though I'm not really sure what it is I'm pleading for.

"Go on, then," he says. And he lets me. Just like that. Like it's a test. Like he's waiting to see if I mess up again. Because then and only then he'll turn me in.

And maybe it's because I want to get caught or maybe it's because I really am the idiot everyone tells me I am, because I don't get five foot before I've failed. Because there, on the mantel above the radiator next to the door, in between a china dog and the phone book, and held down with a mug with a dog on it, is a five pound note.

And without even looking back I pick it up and slip it into my pocket. Because that's what being desperate does to you, doesn't it? When you got nothing you have to survive, and even though it's only a fiver, it buys me one more day and that's all I need.

That's what I say to myself when I shut the door, and that's what I say to myself in bed as I count down the hours and minutes and seconds until Saturday comes and Asha with it.

I just hope she can't see that far inside me to know that I'm the baddie now.

Friday 7 June (6 days late)

It's ink black in my bedroom but I can still see the money. It's like it's made of molten lava or hot coal because, even when I stuff it under my pillow at two in the morning, or down in my trouser pocket when I get up, I can feel it radiating out its bad heat, reminding me what I've done and who I am.

I need to get rid of it then it'll be over – what Perry Fletcher's done to me and what I've done to Otis – so I'm waiting at the gates for him, head down, one good eye up, trying not to stare or get stared at. It's not like they haven't seen anything like it before. Curtis Best came in last term with one ear sewn back on where his nan's dog had bitten it and Perry has a black eye after every pay day. But this is my first time. Whatever bad stuff you could say about Dean – the shouting and the breaking stuff and the names he calls us – he doesn't hit. He's too clever for that, even if he never got his GCSEs.

So everyone's getting a good eyeful – nudging and whispering or just saying it out loud like I'm not even there. The only one who doesn't look is Bradley. He just finds something amazing on his shoe again and keeps on walking.

Perry's late of course. It's five to nine and the playground's empty by the time he saunters up and stubs his cigarette out on the gatepost.

"Waiting for someone?"

I pull the fiver out of my pocket, hold it out like it's burning me, which it is. "Here."

He smirks, snatches it. "Ta."

I plunge my hands back down deep in my

trousers so he can't see they're shaking. Or the black under my fingernails.

"We're done then?"

"Yeah."

I feel a shift in me. Like a tiny ray of sunshine has poked through a gap in the filthy uniform and dirty skin and found a way to warm me.

"Until Monday."

And out goes the light.

"What?" It's a whisper, because the hands around my chest are squeezing it too tight to let anything louder out.

"You thought that was it? Five frigging quid? You really are mental. It's a fiver a week you twat. Until the end of term."

The hands tighten and I think I'm going to do it, I'm going to punch Perry Fletcher. I'm going to do to him what he did to me only worse.

I feel anger then. Boiling up.

"Perry Fletcher. Joe Holt. Over here now."

It's Bloater.

"What's going on?"

Fletcher shrugs.

"Holt?"

"Nothing, sir."

"What happened to you? Your face?"

My brain thinks quick, remembers a football result Bradley was bragging about yesterday. "Fight in the park last night, sir. Over United/Chelsea. Sorry, sir."

"I should think you are. Class, now."

Perry looks back at me. "You stink by the way."

"Fletcher!"

"All right, all right."

Perry's right though. I do stink. When I get to 3B I slink along the wall and sit down at the back, hunch myself over the desk, trying not to move too much so's I don't send smell molecules out. I just need to get through this next hour then I'll go home, I reckon. I'll say I feel ill and go back to the flat and just stay there until Asha turns up tomorrow. She'll know what to do. She knows everything.

But so does someone else.

The bell's gone and I'm hovering, waiting for the others to barge and push their way out into the corridor when Miss Burton looks up from her desk, catches my eye.

"Joe. Wait behind please."

"I . . . I can't, miss. I don't feel so good." And it's true. I feel sick. I hurt all over and I feel sick.

"This won't take long."

I know nothing I say is going to put her off. What is that with women? They don't give up. And sometimes it's good.

But this time it's bad.

She comes to the back of the room, sits down on the desktop in front of me. "What happened to your face?" she asks.

"Nothing," I say. "It was a fight over the football." I laugh, like it's funny.

But she doesn't get the joke.

"I see."

And I know from the way she says it that she does see, only not the kind I was hoping for.

"Have you got your signed letter?"

I feel like something sinks inside me. I can't get anything right. Mental Joe. Can't even remember a stupid signature. "I forgot, miss."

"I think we need to call your mum."

"But—"

"Have you got a mobile?"

I shake my head.

"Fine. We'll use mine." She pulls out an iPhone. Brand new. I know that because the last one got stolen on sports day and sold down the car boot but not before the kid who stole it had sent the texts from Miss Burton's boyfriend round half the school.

"I forgot the number," I say quickly.

"Lucky for you the school has it." She taps in Mum's number off a piece of paper.

Yeah. Lucky for me, I think. I hold my breath, trying really hard not to count the dots on her skirt.

Something's up though. She tries the number again.

"It's dead," she says.

Dead. Of course it is. I knew that. Because there's no way Dean would let her use it in Spain because it'd cost a fortune. He's got a nicked one for that and I don't think even he knows what the number is.

"I think she ran out of credit." The words burst out of my mouth and I breathe clean air back in. Take in great lungfuls of it.

"Joe, what aren't you telling me?"

"Nothing, miss." Everything.

"I'm worried about you. Your face."

For a second I get that feeling again – like she's Asha or Otis – like she's going to help me. But then I remember what Dean says: that people like her, like the social, pretend they're going to help you but it's like they're really good actors or something because they're just pretending, trying to catch you out.

"Don't," I say. "I'm fine, miss."

I watch her take me in: my greasy hair, the black eye and bruised nose with its rim of dried blood. Then her eyes drop to the stain on my blazer.

"Oh, that? Our washing machine's broke," I say quickly. "Dean – my mum's boyfriend – he's gonna fix it."

She looks at me like she's trying to work out which bits of what I've said are true and which are a story.

"OK. But I still need to talk to your mum, or stepdad – what's his name? – Dean?"

I nod. "He's not my stepdad though, miss."

"No. Well, I'm sending a letter and email home asking one of them to see me after school on Monday, OK?"

"OK."

"Go on then."

I go. Out of the classroom, out of the school, out of the gates and home.

But I don't feel relief. I feel like there's a giant

net and it's closing in on me. People are pulling it tighter and tighter – Perry Fletcher, Miss Burton, Jeanie who nearly drops her bottle of Mars milk when she sees me walk past the bookies like something the Staffie dragged in, the shouting man. And then there's Otis. He's one of them now. I made him one of them. It's going to be over soon, I think. Either Mum and Dean will show up or the police will and I'm not even sure which is better any more. Because how's Mum going to explain this one?

This is the end, I know it.

Then I see it, in the gutter outside Crackerjack. A tiny glimmer of gold amongst the dirt and the litter. I crouch painfully to pick it up then hold it there in the palm of my hand, feeling the hard metal of it.

It's a one pound coin.

Just a one pound coin. And I know there's not much you can do with a pound. You can't get a lifetime's supply of happiness or chocolate or even dog food like Jeanie won once in a radio phone-in. She didn't even have a dog but she said it was the winning that counts. Plus Dean sold it for her down the well and she got thirty quid in the end.

You can't get trainers or a pizza or even four thousand packets of Tic Tacs.

But it's a pound. And when you've got less than nothing it's a whole lot of something. It's a discount loaf of bread and a Freddo bar.

And, more than that, it's a sign, a reminder. That tomorrow Asha is coming. And that she'll know what to do.

Somehow, she'll take all this world of wrong and make it right.

Saturday 8 June (7 days late)

I use the last of the washing–up liquid and scrub at my hair and my body, trying to get the blood and the sweat and the dirt out. I still look a mess when I'm done but I don't smell so bad. At least, not above the rest of the flat. I've opened the windows but it doesn't seem to make a difference. Just adds bus fumes and rotting bins to the staleness and the sick in here.

I eat bread and brown sauce; four slices of it, same as last night. It's weird how good something like that tastes when it's all you've got. I can't wash the plate up when I'm done but I don't feel bad. Because Asha is coming.

She's late. She doesn't show up until half past four and by then the feast is all dried up and the balloons have popped and I'm stood there like an idiot.

"My mum, innit," she says as she follows me back to the sofa, flops into the hollow. "She said she was gonna bring me this morning but then some girl gets herself arrested at Finsbury Park Tube and she has to go and get her out and Ellis can't bring me because he's playing badminton. I mean, who plays badminton?"

"I dunno."

"You angry or something?" She leans back on the saggy cushion, looks at me sideways.

I shrug. Am I? No, I think. Not angry. Just disappointed. And scared. And hungry. And sorry. And all these things, all these emotions fighting for space inside my head and the only way I can order them is by the counting only I can't do that in front of her because then she'll realise I'm mental, and anyway I shouldn't need to because she's the one who's supposed to make it all better, only why isn't she?

"Joe?"

"I—" But I don't get any further than that because all the feelings have started to leak out through my eyes. I'm crying. And I'm scared it's going to be like last time, with the snot and the shaking. But then I feel her fingers on my arm, then her arms around my chest and she's holding me. Properly holding me, so that my head's on her shoulder, my lips on her neck.

"It's OK," she's saying. "It's gonna be OK, Joe."

I pull my head up so's I can see her. "Is it?" I'm saying silently.

She nods.

And then she does something. Something so incredible and impossible and wondrous that for a second I think I'm so gone I'm hallucinating.

She kisses me. Not just on the cheek like Mum does, or slobbery drunk so her tongue slides off like Jeanie, but on the lips. A real kiss. And I know I'm not imagining things because when I kiss her back she lets me. And it's like her mouth is as blessed as her fingers, because when it meets mine, she sort of takes away all the bad, sucks it out inside of her and dissolves it.

Which doesn't sound beautiful when you say it like that. But that's exactly what it is.

And when it's finally over I don't feel dirty like I used to when I looked at the photos on Bradley's phone or see the Year 11s snogging round the back of the labs. I feel clean, and new and strong. I feel like she's changed me, given me some of her powers. So that I can do anything, say anything.

"I'm in trouble," I tell her.

"I know."

"So what do I do?"

She thinks, her forefinger tracing the edge of the

stain on the cushion. Keeps doing it, thinking harder, more.

"Ash?"

"You got to go," she says finally.

"Where?" I ask.

"I dunno. Dean's family? It's got to be better than this, surely."

I remember the smell and the dog poo. And the staring at the walls and the shouting. I shake my head. "No."

She thinks again, quicker this time. "Your nan's then. It's not you and her fallen out, is it. It's your mum. And when your nan finds out what's happened she'll be all crying and saying sorry and giving you money and stuff. Trust me, I've seen it."

"I told you, I don't know where she lives. Not really."

Then I remember something. Something else at the back of Mum's drawer. That postcard. The one she rowed with Carl over then carried around anyway like it's some kind of magic ring.

"Hang on." I run to the bedroom, yank open the drawer so that a tangle of knickers and bra straps falls on my feet. I kick them away. Let them clean them up. When they get back. If they get back.

It's there.

On the front is a beach that you know's been messed with so's it doesn't look real: the sand bright yellow, the sea turquoise, people in swimming costumes the colour of jewels or tropical birds: ruby red, parakeet green. It's paradise. Or as good as.

And this paradise has an address and all.

"Twelve Seacrest Road, Penzance, Cornwall," I read.

"Well that's it, then," she says. Like I'm Indiana Jones and I've found the arc of the covenant. "You got to go to Penzance."

But Indiana had gadgets and a rich dad and a beautiful girl by his side. I have Asha, but she's not going to come with me, is she. "How though?"

"Train, duh."

"I don't mean that, I know there's trains. I mean how'm I supposed to pay for it?"

"I could ask Otis for a lend," she says. "He's good like that—"

"No," I say quickly. "I can't." Not when I've already had money off him when I didn't even ask and he didn't offer.

"You could sell something," she tries.

"Like what?"

"Xbox, PlayStation, TV." She lists off the only good stuff left, the only good stuff we had in the first place.

I try to imagine myself going into the Well, offering them to the Dooleys or Jeanie. Getting twenty quid for the lot if I'm lucky. That's not enough to get as far as Reading. I need way more than that. I need . . .

"I need to show you something," I say.

"What?" Her cat's eyes are bright, alert now.

I feel weird as I stand up, wobbly. Like it's not me who leads her to the bathroom, not me who takes the lid off the cistern, not me who lifts out the bag, dripping water over the lino, pulls off the plastic to show her what's inside.

But it is me, it's me and her and two thousand pounds, and it's there for the taking. And as I see the look on Asha's face I realise that this, not the postcard, this is the Ark of the Covenant. This is pirate's gold and the crown jewels and buried treasure all in one.

"Oh. My. God," she says. "For real."

For real.

We count it twice. It's all there still. Dean hasn't touched it. Two thousand pounds, in twenty piles of one hundred pounds each. Round and neat numbers.

"How much d'you reckon I need?" I ask.

"All of it, duh."

"What?" It can't cost that much to Penzance. Not even in first class.

"Not just for the train," she says. "For stuff. Food. Hotel, even. I mean what if your nan's away on one of them coach trips and you have to wait a couple of days or something?"

I try to picture it. A thirteen-year-old in jeans and a T-shirt with a plastic bag trying to check in to the Grand or the Plaza or whatever the hotels are called down there. It's not going to happen. It's not going to happen because my nan is going to be there, in the blue sky with the beach behind her and a flock of parakeets in the trees, and she's going to see me and look all funny at first, like she knows who I am but can't quite place me. Then she'll realise. And she'll open her arms and say my name. "Joe, Joe . . ."

"Joe?"

I close my eyes to get rid of the picture. "Huh?"

"When are you going to do it? Go, I mean."

"I dunno." Now? No. Too soon. I need a plan. I need to work out where I'm going. I need to go to the library and get maps and train times and all that kind of stuff. I know Huck and Tom never had any of that, but they didn't live in Peckham.

"Monday?"

She nods.

"Shall I—"

But whatever word or words are about to come out, whatever plan or scheme or grand idea she's thought up is batted away, pushed back down and stoppered up because we've forgotten about something. Someone.

Otis.

"Asha?"

He's at the door. Listening. Waiting.

"I know you in there, girl."

"In a minute," she calls.

"Not a minute, now."

She stands but I grab her sleeve, try to pull her back.

"You can't," I say. "If you open the door . . . " and then I stop, because there's so many things now – he'll see the money; he'll know for sure Dean's not back; he'll see how bad the flat is; he'll ask me where that fiver is.

"Here." She pushes the money under the sofa. "It'll be fine. I like you so he likes you. End of."

But she doesn't know what I've done. Not yet. She might not like me then.

"Asha!" I say. But it's too late. The door's open and he's inside. In the flat. Looking, peering into the gloom.

Then he closes his eyes and it's like he's preparing himself, garnering all his strength like a boxer before a fight or a lion about to pounce.

Like Dean when Mum answers back and he looks down and shakes his head and she knows she's for it any second.

Otis opens his eyes and I wait for it. Wait for him to explode, the bad words and the threats flying out like sticks and stones to break your bones.

But when he says them they're not hard or sharp. They're soft. And sad.

"Where is she, boy?"

"Who?" I say, stupidly, playing for time.

"You know who. I ask you before and you don't tell me. Your mum."

"She's ill," Asha says quickly. "She's in bed, she can't be disturbed."

Otis shakes his head. "No more lies, girl. I know she not here."

"But—"

"No buts, Asha. When they back, boy? Her and that . . . that man."

"I—I . . . I don't know. Tomorrow, I think. Yeah, Tomorrow."

"I don't believe you people," he says. "Leavin' a chile alone." He's shaking his head at it all. At this sorry picture we make.

"I'm not a child. I'm thirteen," I protest.

"And look what thirteen got you," he says. I don't need to see where he's looking to know what he means – this no-electricity no-food no-mum world.

"She back tomorrow you say?"

I nod.

"If they not back by tomorrow night then I'm calling police," he says. "A boy can't live like this. He need folk, nah? Kith and kin. He need family."

I nod.

"Come, Asha."

She doesn't look at me. Just follows him. I don't get to kiss her. I don't even get to say goodbye.

It's all right for her. She's got family. Even if her mum loves Ellis and her job more than Asha, she wouldn't go and leave her. And even if she did, Asha's got Otis.

But me. Well, I'm going to get me a family. I'm going to catch a train to paradise and find my own folk. Tomorrow.

It's decided now. That's when I go. I'll leave early. Seven. Then I've got all day before Otis knocks and finds they're not back and I'm gone.

The phone rings seventeen times between 20.47 and 00.13. I don't answer it though because I know who it is and I don't want to talk to him. Because

I know what he's after now and it's not Dean, it's what Dean's got. Only Dean hasn't got it any more, I have. And he knows it.

At 01.22 the buzzer on the door goes and I hear him shouting up only it's not Dean's name he's shouting, it's mine: "Joe Holt, you little shit," he yells up. "I know you're in there. I know what you got." But Mrs Joyful King opens her window and tells him she's calling the police if he doesn't stop his racket so he does. Only not without saying he'll be back in the morning. But I know he's drunk on beer from the way he slurred "little shit" and I know how late you sleep with that inside you and so by the time he wakes up he'll have a headache and I'll be gone. And I feel golden then, golden.

I don't need timetables or maps after all.

I'm Huck. I'm lighting out for the territory.

I'm lighting out for paradise.

Sunday 9 June (8 days late)

I don't sleep so much even with the golden feeling inside. But I'm not worried; I'll sleep on the train I reckon. I mean, how many hours is it to Penzance? Could be five, could be fifteen even. Maybe not that many, but enough. Enough hours and enough miles away from all of this – the shouting man, Perry Fletcher and his fists and his words, Bradley and his silence and looking at his shoes, Jeanie and her drunk kisses, and this crappy flat with its stinking fridge and no hot water and stains and crack and the hollow in the sofa from Dean's useless arse, and the massive gaping hole where Mum should be.

The only good thing I'm leaving behind when you really think about it is Asha.

I'm going to write to her though. Send her a postcard with a too-bright beach on it and my new address and then she'll come to stay in the holidays. I'll meet her off the train and we can get ice cream and sit on the beach and Nan can take a photo of us and I'll stick it on a fridge with a magnet so that she's always with me even when she's not.

I keep thinking about her. About what she did, what we did. But I have to stop because it's making me feel hot and weird so that my heart goes too quick like a mouse's and I lose count of the beats.

I look at my watch. It's 6.57. Three minutes to go.

I can't sit down any more, have to walk up and down to get rid of the buzzing in my legs. It's four steps across the floor each way and I do it thirty times which makes 240 steps. But I don't like that number so I do another ten steps to take it to 250, which feels better even though I've ended up in the middle of the room.

I check my watch again. 6.59.

I count the seconds down now.

6.59.14

I pick my rucksack up, feel its weight pull when I sling it on my back. It's funny, I thought I'd travel light, like Dick Whittington only going the wrong way, with just a hankie and a hunk of bread. Only I didn't have a hunk I had sliced white so I've got two brown sauce sandwiches, and some clothes, plus the money, and after that I couldn't fit anything else in.

6.59.48

This is it.

I walk to the door.

6.59.54

I twist the handle, my fingers trembling, my

heart still keeping mouse-time while the watch seems to tick over in slow motion.

6.59.57

6.59.58

And then I hear it.

"Joe?"

"Asha?"

I pull the door open wide and she's there, in a white dress with a pair of red shoes in her hand and the sun behind her like a halo.

She's crept silently. Not even slid in her socks but stealthy, on tiptoes like a spy or a cartoon burglar.

I go to speak, have to ask her a hundred questions: what she's doing here and why and how and what if Otis finds out, but she puts her finger to her lips.

"Not now, innit," she whispers.

"But you can't—"

"I can. And I am."

And just like that it's decided. That I'm not a

lone adventurer any more. I'm not on my own, I've got my sidekick, my beautiful girl. We are Huck and Tom, Tom and Becky, Batman and Catwoman. Wherever I go, she'll come too and we'll never be apart. My heart thuds so loud, so heavy I think she'll hear it, think Otis will hear it.

"Thank—"

But that's all I manage because her lips are on mine again, and my head is so full of her there's no room for thinking or worrying and my heart stops its mouse-time march and dances instead, and then my legs follow it as she's pulling me down the stairs, one, two at a time, flying to the door, to the world, to a new life.

"Wait," I gasp, pull her back.

"What? Come on. We have to go." She's impatient now, looking up at the windows, watching to see who's watching us. But Mrs Joyful King's curtains are closed, the broken blind in the students' house hanging down to hide what's inside and out.

"There's something I need to do," I explain. "It won't take long."

"Joe!" She calls after me but I don't answer. I have to do this. This one thing. She'd understand, if she knew. Just like Otis will understand when he sees it.

I slip it under his door.

Just the one note. A twenty to replace the five I took.

With one word written above the Queen's face in black biro.

"Sorry." Because I am, I really am. Because he showed me more kindness with that bowl of water and the bottle of TCP than Dean's done in two years. Because I wish he was my sort-of-granddad, like Asha.

I wish he was my dad.

But he's not. And like Jeanie says, if wishes were horses, beggars would ride. So there's no point wishing or even wondering. I just have to walk.

So I'm gone again, and this time it's for good.

Because by the time my watch says 7.09.48 we're on the back seats of the number 36 heading down the High Road to freedom.

It's like I'm drinking it in. This last look. With Asha holding my hand I take it in – what I see and what she sees – like a photograph so I won't forget: the drunks at Camberwell, asleep now in the doorway of the Silver Buckle; the cricket ground with the walls all covered in leaves like you must be playing in a perfect round forest; the sweep of the river as it curves its muddy way round to Battersea.

The woman two seats in front who puts on perfect red lipstick in the half-reflection of the grimy window; the man at the back who eats a McMuffin like it's the saddest thing he ever tasted; the kid in black with the hat pulled down so you can't see his eyes so it's like he's reading through a criss-cross of black wool.

"He's a poet," Asha says. "A vampire poet who

lives in an ivory tower with no windows and if he takes his hat off he'll turn into a puff of smoke."

I think he lives in a tower block and smokes too much puff because I can smell it on him all thick and sweet, but I don't tell her that because I like her story better. She's good at stories, making stuff up. You could call it lies, I guess, but there's so much detail that that doesn't seem good enough for it. Tales, that's what they are, tall tales. Like the one she told Otis on the note she left on the kitchen table. That she's remembered she got invited to go up West with some friend and she needed to go home to get her blue dress because this girl is going to wear her white one and they don't want to look like twins because that is so last year. She says if she makes it about girl stuff he won't call anyone because men don't like to even think about dresses or make-up or tampons or stuff and I remember Dean and the drawer and I reckon she's right and we're safe. That we've got a good ten hours before Asha's mum shows up at Otis's and they put two and two together and get a whole lot less than four.

I thought it would be like it is on the news, all bustling with hundreds of people with suitcases and umbrellas and running to get through the barriers at the last minute, but Paddington's still and quiet on a Sunday morning. Not even all the shops are open, just two Asian guys flipping burgers, and a pale girl with a ponytail eating a double chocolate chip at the cookie stand, and twenty-seven people sitting on silver benches drinking coffee and Coke and watching the departure board tick over.

"Too late for the eight o'clock, innit," Asha says.

"We've got five minutes," I say. I just want to get on the train. Because even though Asha's story is good, what if Otis can see – like she can – and sees right through the note and the story and calls the police and they block all the roads and the trains or something. I tell Asha that but she laughs, says they only do that for terrorists.

"Anyway, we've got to buy tickets. And I'm hungry. And I need a magazine because there's this new one and you get a free nail varnish and it's worth eight quid and the magazine only costs three pound fifty so even if you don't like the magazine, which I do, you've still saved yourself, what?"

"Four pound fifty," I say without thinking.

"Exactly. So we can't get the eight o'clock, we'll get the eight fifty-seven."

And that's that.

You'd think buying two train tickets was easy when you've got two thousand pounds in your bag and you don't care whether you're in first class or the quiet carriage and you're never coming back, but it's not.

The man's old with thin hair and yellow fingers and a look at me and Asha like we smell bad. We should have used the machine, I think. I said that to Asha and all but she said they always mess up and once one ate her tenner and she never got it back because they were in a hurry. I say to her that we could lose a hundred quid and it wouldn't matter but she's having none of it so the yellow-fingered man it is.

Asha wants to do the talking because she says girls look older than boys even when they're not, plus he won't question her because of the girl stuff thing and when I go to argue I hear my voice crack so I just let her anyway.

"Two to Penzance," she says and does this smile so her white teeth shine out.

The old guy doesn't smile back but I can see his teeth are all yellow like his fingers and there's black in between like someone's drawn them in with a felt tip.

"Single or return?" he asks with a voice that's as thin as his hair and his teeth.

"Return," she shoots back, not missing a beat.

But we're not coming back, I think. At least I'm not. So, what? She's just dropping me off? Like I'm some kid who needs a chaperone? My legs feel weak again as I get this picture in my head of me standing on a platform while she just stays at the window, waves and the train shunts backwards, like rewind on a DVD so she's sucked all the way back up the track to here again.

But then I feel her fingers reach out and tangle themselves with mine, squeeze them, and then I feel it, what she's trying to say. That it's better like that. Then he won't think we're running away. He'll think we're just on a day trip or something. Brilliant. She's brilliant.

"When are you coming back?" The man says the words like he's a robot. Like he repeats the same questions on a five-minute cycle all day every day, maybe even at home because he can't stop himself.

"Today," I blurt. Because it'll be cheaper that way. I remember seeing that on a TV programme once. That it's even cheaper than a single. I feel like I've won the prize then. That I've finally got something right and I'm top of the class, not even the remedial class but the A1 stream who mostly live on the Grove and get to go to university.

But I feel Asha jab me with a bony elbow and I know I've messed up even before he says it.

"You're having a laugh, aren't you? Penzance and back in a day? What you going to do? Take a quick shufti at the station café and come right back?"

"He meant same day next week," Asha says, rolling her eyes like she's on his side. Like she can a have a laugh with him at the mental boy.

I feel my eyes sting but I can't do that now – cry, I mean – or he'll know something's up so I count the stickers on the window between us: eighteen – a good number – two times nine – and then it's OK again because I remember that it's just a story to fool him.

"Two hundred and fifty-four pounds."

"A hundred and twenty-seven each? For a child?" I say.

I've done it again. Blown it. Who's gonna let two kids get the train. The whole point was to pretend we were sixteen, that's what Asha said on the bus. Just look bored, she said. But I look anything but. I look scared and cross and lost and like a kid, a dumb kid who's running away with a stolen fortune and a sandwich that's leaked brown sauce on his socks and pants.

But the yellow man doesn't press a red button or pick up the phone. He doesn't even look up from the computer. Just says, "Got ID?"

Dean's right, I think. No one cares. No one gives a shit. You could be bleeding or dancing naked and they'd cross the road on the other side. London's like the opposite of school where everything counts. Out here I'm not Mental Joe, I'm just another customer who's taking up too much time.

"Sorry, I forgot."

Asha sucks her teeth.

"What about you?" he asks her.

She pushes over her Oyster card and he half glances at it.

"All right. So that's one adult, one child. That's ... " He presses some buttons. "A hundred and ninety pounds and fifty pence."

I take a handful of notes out of my pocket and count out ten, hand them to Asha who pushes them through the plastic grille.

"Rob a bank, did ya?" the man laughs.

"Maybe," says Asha.

He tuts then and I think he's thinking, *Kids. It wasn't like that in my day.* Because that's what old people always say, isn't it. But what about Tom and Huck, then? They were kids and they did bad stuff sometimes and that was the olden days even if it was in a book.

But even though yellow man reckons we might be criminals he gives us the tickets, which just goes to show that I was right all along. We were right all along.

"Told you, didn't I?" Asha says. "Piece of cake."

"Yeah," I say. "Easy as pie."

"Sweet as a nut," she comes back.

But I can't think of another one so we just go to get breakfast.

It's like when you take the top off something and everything spills out. Or like those crisps – once you pop you just can't stop. Because now that we've bought tickets we start buying all kinds of stuff. Not just burgers and chips and Pepsi, not just three magazines and a word-search book. But stuff we don't need, don't even want, or not until now. We get a Paddington Bear key ring and a calculator pen and a glow-in-the-dark rubber set. We get two kinds of chocolate and four kinds of chewing gum and candy floss in a bag like we're at the fair. We even get a bunch of flowers – peonies, it says – for Nan. Then we sit down on the silver bench and eat and read and paint our nails Fancy Flamingo – mine and all – and wait for the clock to tick round another forty-three minutes. And all the while I'm thinking how lucky I am, after all. That despite everything, the no money and the mum who ran away, I got Asha, and now I'm going to get my nan back so I'll have a proper family. Maybe she can come and look after me, and her and Otis can be friends, and Mrs Joyful King too. Or we can all move to Cornwall and the parakeets will come too, they'll flock to live in the cliffs and dunes and we can all have a taste of paradise.

The station's busier now. Trains have come in from Reading and Cardiff and Heathrow Airport, opening their doors and letting out streams of people like insects who scurry down more tunnels to the Tube or out to the taxi rank and buses. The seats are crowded too. A bunch of kids with two mums are behind us playing I–Spy. Two rows down is a boy with a lightning streak shaved in his head. Like mine should have been. I glance at Asha, seeing if she's watching him, but she's looking at pictures of some actress's bottom which is too fat according to the magazine because it's got that massive red pen mark round it again, like when you've messed up your homework. I wonder what bits of me need a red pen round them. My head for a start.

"How come . . . " I start.

Asha looks up. "Huh?"

"I . . . " I don't want to say it. But I need to know. Because I've tried to work it out. Every day since the Rye. Just, what it is she sees, when she sees me. Because as far as I can tell there's not much there to get all excited about. I don't look like anyone in her magazines. And I don't look like that kid over there. I don't even look like Perry Fletcher. "What do you think . . . " The words stick in my throat like dried seeds. Like they're digging in, and getting them out is painful. "About me, I mean?" I manage.

She frowns at first. Like she's never thought of it before. And now that she does it's not good news.

"Truth," I say then. Because I don't want one of her stories.

"OK, truth." She shrugs, like it's nothing. Like

deciding on which is just like flipping a coin. But truth is everything. It changes everything.

"I think you're weird—"

There it is.

"—in a good way," she carries on. "And I like your eyes. I like brown eyes. They're more . . . " She searches for the word she's read on page twenty-five somewhere. "Sensual."

I do this strangled cough noise when she says that. Like I'm choking on it. But she doesn't stop. She's on a roll now, saying all the things she can see. And there's so much. Stuff I've never noticed. Stuff even Mum's never noticed, or not said anyway.

"Yeah. And when you smile it's mostly on one side. And you have really nice lips. And you're skinny only not too skinny. I mean, you're dead good-looking if you think about it, only you don't know it. Which is kind of good. Only mental. Because you only got to look in the mirror, innit."

"You want to know what I like about you?" I blurt. Because words are queuing up now, ready to push their way out like passengers off a train.

"Uh-huh?"

"I like your eyes too, because they're like cat's eyes. Only it's not the way they look *to* me, it's they way they look *at* me, you know? The way they look at the world. I like that. I like the way you see the world."

For a minute I reckon she's going to be disappointed. Bradley says all girls get hacked off if you don't talk about their lips or their legs or their boobs every five minutes.

But Asha's not all girls.

So Asha smiles, and eats another French fry and leans her head on my shoulder.

Because she knows what I mean.

And that's what I mean.

The departure board clicks over like a domino shuffle or a Mexican wave, all the destinations and times whirring and clacking and coming up new. The train is boarding on platform 1.

"That's us," I say.

We're off. We're off to see the wizard. I remember Carl singing the song one Christmas when that film was on the telly. And him and Mum had had too many Snowballs and they got up and did this mad dance and then they pulled me up with them and then we were all singing it, "We're off to see the wizard, the wonderful Wizard of Oz."

Only instead of a yellow brick road we've got silver train tracks, and there's no tin man or lion or scarecrow. Just me and Asha in her red shoes.

"I feel sick," says Asha. But she's grinning, and I know it's that fairground sick again, the excited kind, the kind you want to keep coming.

"Me too," I say. Truth. I feel it and all. Like I'm on the top of a roller coaster and as soon as the guard blows the whistle we'll soar down the rails, leaving everything behind us in the wind. Her mum, Dean, Perry Fletcher: all of them.

And that's when it happens. I don't believe it at first. Because I never seen it, not even on *EastEnders*. But there's this voice, quiet at first, because it's far away, then louder, rising above the tinny announcer and the chatter of crowds and the clatter of trains. "Asha," it calls. "Ash-aaaaaa."

She turns, her mouth open, eyes so wide I can see their whiteness, their shape like marbles in her skull. "Otis," she says, like she can't believe it. Like it can't be true.

But it is.

He's on the far side of the station, by the bagel stand, but getting closer every second, running like he's got tigers behind him, or soldiers with machine guns. He pushes people out of the way and a kid falls over and starts crying. He turns and says something over his shoulder but he doesn't stop. He's not going to stop. Which means we have to . . .

"Run!" Asha turns and pulls me after her and then we're helter-skeltering through people too.

Like we're in some giant Xbox and every time you bump into someone you lose five points. What's the game though? What's the aim of the game now? Where are we running to?

I feel Asha knock into something, someone, and then she's on the ground and I try to pull her up but she's crying now.

"Come on," I beg. "Otis, he's—"

But I stop. Because then I see something. No, someone. Someone else has followed us here. Or was waiting. And I hear him in my head before he says the words out loud: "Joe Holt, you little shit."

Shouting man. Mickey Dooley.

I don't know how, but he's here. Maybe he followed us. Or followed Otis. But now there's two baddies. And the net is wider and it's closing tighter.

"Just go," Asha pleads. "I'll be fine. Go on. Go!"

And this time I'm gone. I don't know where I'm running. I'm on a platform now. Don't know how I got here. People are pouring out of a train, dodging past me, calling me an idiot under their breath, and worse. But no one stops me. No one reaches out to catch me. I'm still winning the game.

I'm nearly through the crowd and I can see light, daylight past the arched brick walls, can see the end of the platform. But then what? I think. Then what happens.

I should turn, I think, like maybe there's a way off to the left. I glance, but there's just an office or something, which looks locked. The only other choice is back where I came from. But I know what's back there and not even knowing Asha's there makes me want to take that route.

So I only have one choice if you think about it. I have to keep going. I have to run until there's nothing left, until there's nothing under my feet any more except air and sky. Then I'll fly. I'll be like a parakeet, I reckon. Or Icarus. That's it. The man who made his own wings and flew to the sun.

But as I watch my left foot leave the platform

and step into nothingness, I feel a hand grab my rucksack and pull me, and as I tumble backwards the bag bursts open and a shower of twenty and ten pound notes flutters into the air around me like feathers as I hit the cold, hard concrete. And I remember the rest of that story: Icarus fell.

And I know it's all over.

Friday 5 July

It was stupid, really. Mental, like they always said. I was never going anywhere. There's nothing at the end of the platforms. No paradise, no pot of gold. Just stones and the chewed-up toilet paper and poo that gets flushed out of the carriages. I was lucky really, that Otis got me when he did 'cause I could have landed on a live rail or something. Then I'd have been as fried as our skinny chips. As it was I just got concussion.

If this had been a film, or one of Asha's stories,

I'd have opened my eyes and there'd have been my mum. Her and Dean would've had a fight and she'd have said he was no good and she'd have left him for ever in Spain and come to rescue me instead, her handsome prince. She'd have been getting off the train from Heathrow when she heard Otis shouting out my name. And then it would go all slow motion and the sound would be like in a swimming pool – all echoey and strange. She'd have dropped her suitcase and her duty free and there'd be this slow smash of bottles and a straw donkey or something would've rolled across the tiles. Then she'd have run, her hair all out behind her and her arms towards me. And I'd have stood up and seen her through some smoke and said, "Mummy, oh my mummy," like in that film about the kids on the railway.

But this is real life. So, when I opened my eyes, there's this crowd of faces staring down at me, blocking the light, and in them Otis, and Asha.

She's knelt over me with her eyes all red and her

face all stained from her make-up and this bit of snot hanging off her nose. She looks beautiful right then. More beautiful than she's ever looked. And she smiles and rockets go off in my head one after the other and I think I'm invincible and can stand up and carry her off like a hero in a film. But when I lift my head I just throw up on the platform. And after that everything does go slow and blurry, and I'm not sure what bits are real and which are just in my head. But I do know this: that when I wake up again, I'm in a bed in a hospital and Asha's gone and there's this nurse and a woman with grey hair in a grey suit, in fact she's all grey, even her skin. And I know who she is, and I know where she's taking me.

So that's where I am now: Forest Hill, which makes it sound like it's in the middle of the country with foxes and kestrels and pine trees, but it's just more kebab shops and buses and blocks of flats.

And this place.

And the O'Connell brothers were right, it's not like *Tracy Beaker*. There's no cupcakes and food fights and days out to the beach. But it's not as bad as I thought either. I mean, no one's tried to smack me one yet. And there's chips and sausages and stuff like that for dinner. And the boy in the room next to mine – Geno – he gave me a lend of his phone yesterday and I beat him at Angry Birds and he didn't call me a twat or try to break anything.

But he's at school at the moment and he's taken his phone with him so instead I'm reading all about Tom and Huck because they have a copy here, and Keith who works nights says it doesn't matter if I've already read it because sometimes old stories are the best, they're comfort, like an old blanket. And as I turn the pages, I think he's right, and I think I'm glad she's coming after all. And maybe one day I can read a bit to her, just because I can.

At first I told them I didn't want to see her. Not today and not ever again. But Julia – my social worker – she says it doesn't work like that. She says it's just a visit and it doesn't have to be for long and it's OK to tell her how I feel, even if it means shouting. Only she knows what she did was wrong, and this is about making it right, starting from now.

Only she's still not here. All I can see out the window is the 176 bus coming from Penge and the 24-hour garage and an old woman looking into the postbox like it might have a monster inside that's eaten her letter. Maybe it has. Maybe that's why Asha's not written back. I sent her a letter last week – well to Otis's, because I don't know her own address – telling her where I am and saying she can come and see me if she likes. But maybe it never got there. Maybe it got lost – they lose thousands of letters every year according to Julia. Or maybe it's stuck under the doormat, or Mrs Joyful King has stacked it with the pizza leaflets by mistake. Or perhaps Otis gave it to Asha's mum and she put it in the bin with the rubbish saying "good riddance".

There's a bus coming up the other way now. Up from the West End, and Elephant and Camberwell. Two men get off it, both in vests and all shiny with sweat in the heat. Then a mum in shorts, only she can't get her pushchair down and the kid is crying and kicking so another woman, all skinny in a red dress with long blonde hair leans down to help her lift it on to the pavement.

It's not until she stands up straight again that I realise who it is.

My heart does that thing: goes fast and hard like I'm about to fall off something, or get hit, and my stomach rolls and I'm back at the fairground again, my carriage teetering at the top of the roller coaster. Then she looks up at the window, and stares, and then her mouth moves into a sort of scared smile, and the train plunges forward and me with it, out my room, and down the stairs and out the front door right into her arms.

"I'm sorry," she's saying into my hair. "I'm sorry, I'm sorry, I'm sorry."

"Me too," I say back, only you can't hear it so well because I'm shaking and the words get lost in the sound of a sob.

But she catches them still, pulls away, holds me by the shoulders. Her eyes are red and there's black down her cheeks from her make-up, and some snot as well, and she looks a bit like she's in a horror film or something. "Why're you sorry?" she asks.

And I think of all the things I should have done different. Shouldn't have left the Xbox on. Shouldn't have eaten the curry. Shouldn't have left the twenty pounds for Otis because then he'd never have worked out what was going on. Should have got a taxi, not the 36 bus, then Otis's mate Charley wouldn't have called him saying why the hell is Asha going to Paddington with some boy on a Sunday, why she not in church. Should have seen Mickey Dooley sitting on the wall opposite the flats and gone another way, or changed buses at the last minute so's he got trapped and had to watch us through the glass as we waved goodbye.

Only I'm not sorry, I think. Not really. Because I did some things right. Because I took the money, and, even though some of it got lost and some of it got taken, there was still nearly eighteen hundred pounds when the police collected it all. And they came to the hospital and asked where it came from and I told them, so Dean got caught and charged for benefit fraud over all his "little jobs" and for something to do with drugs and all. He got ten years. It would have been longer but he grassed up Chinese Tony and Mickey Dooley so they're inside, which means at least ten years of peace, or eight with good behaviour.

And because, even if I'd got to Cornwall, my nan wouldn't have been there anyway. The police tried to contact her from hospital because Mum's phone was still dead so I said Nan was my family. They had to send a Cornish copper round to 12 Seacrest Road only the lady who lives there now – Mrs Peasland – said she moved to Spain last year. Funny how things work out, isn't it.

And because this – right here on the pavement with the sound of all the traffic and the hot sun on our heads and Julia waiting inside with a cup of tea and a can of Coke and biscuits on a plate – this isn't so bad.

"I don't know," I say. "I'm . . . I'm just . . . "

But I don't finish the sentence, because she's holding me again and telling me this time it'll be different, I'll see, now that he's gone, now that she's kicking the drink. She says she realised it in Spain. That she tried to come home on her own that first Saturday only he'd hidden her passport so's she couldn't. And that when she saw the police at the arrivals gate at Heathrow nine days later she said it was like seeing angels because she knew then it would all stop.

And I know it's not a film or a story. I know it's real life, and promises are nothing but words and wishes, and if wishes were horses, beggars would ride. But I believe her. Because you have to, don't you. You have to believe in the good stuff, in the fairy tale. I don't mean the dragons and the dwarves and the princes, but the happy ever after, the paradise.

That's what I tell myself every day. So what if we never made it to Penzance? So what if we never even made it past Paddington? Every Sunday, when she visits, we go up the Rye – me and Mum. And Asha if she's about and Otis too if he's not working.

And on sunny days – when the parakeets swoop and soar, and the rocks stretch out their legs and turn into turtles, and Asha traces circles on my jeans and arms and cheeks – it feels enough like paradise to me.

Acknowledgements

Thank you to my agents Sarah Molloy and Julia Churchill, who saw an oak in my acorn of an idea that afternoon in Paddington; to Karen Ball for believing in me and Joe; to Helen Stringfellow and Catherine Bruton for kind and clever words, and for always seeing the good in the world; to their two Joes for lending me their name; and to Peckham Rye, which gave me eleven years of almost-paradise, with parakeets, Ninja Turtles and gold glinting the gutter.